A SIP OF RIO

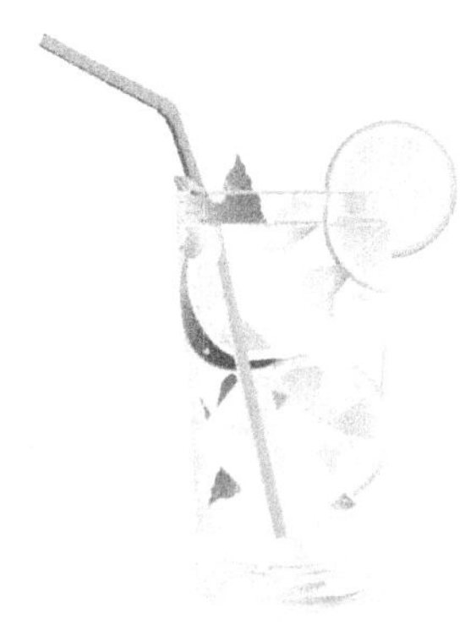

TEODORA KOSTOVA

ISBN: 9781728604015

Edited by Kameron Mitchell
Proofread by Lydia Bird and Vicki Potter
Cover art by Jay Aheer at Simply Defined Art

Disclaimer

This is a work of fiction. All names, places and incidents are either the product of the author's imagination, or are used fictitiously.

Chapter one

Blaine signed the divorce papers and threw the pen on the table, a bit more forcefully than necessary. It bounced and rolled off the edge, landing on the hardwood floor with a dull thud.

Blaine didn't move to pick it up. He stared at his signature, still unable to believe he was divorced at twenty nine. What a fucking joke. Linda, his *ex-wife*, was probably opening the champagne right now, even though it was barely lunch time. Blaine didn't feel like celebrating. He felt like the rock around his neck had finally been cut, letting him breathe freely and find his way back to the shore. And yet, celebrating was the last thing on his mind.

He'd loved her. So damn much.

It was done. No point in looking back, wondering what he could have done differently. Blaine had done that plenty of times during their two years of 'trial separation' and then again while the divorce was being finalised. It had been a long time since Linda had left him, and it was time he moved on. She surely had.

Pushing his chair back, Blaine stood up and headed to the coffee maker. It might be lunch time for everyone else, but for him it was barely the crack of dawn. A radio DJ, Blaine rarely came home from work before 3 AM. His show ran every week day from midnight to 2 AM, and was hugely popular despite the late hour.

A smile played on Blaine's lips as he watched the dark liquid fill the coffee pot, the aroma of the strong Kenyan coffee filling his small kitchen, and thought about calling Hayden to tell him the news.

Blaine's best friend Hayden Frost was a freelance investigative journalist writing for nearly every leading LGBT publication in the world. Fluent in four languages, Hayden could take his pick from any magazine, newspaper, or respected website, but he believed, as a gay man, he should support the media aimed at LGBT people. Blaine didn't necessarily agree – his opinion had always been that in order to achieve full equality, the divide between gay and straight had to be erased. Blur the lines, so to speak.

He firmly believed that was the way to move past all segregation and prejudice. Blaine'd argued about this exact issue with Hayden the first day they'd met in college, nearly ten years ago. You can't have it both ways, Hayden'd said.

Yet another thing blamed on Blaine's bisexuality.

Oddly enough, they'd been inseparable since then. Well, inseparable wasn't the right word, considering Hayden rarely stayed in London for more than two weeks at a time. As Blaine poured the steaming hot coffee into a mug, he wondered what the time was in Boston right now. Hayden had gone to America a couple of weeks ago, chasing a lead on a blackmailing scandal involving a very conservative American politician and a young British actor.

Deciding to send a text instead of calling, and hoping he wouldn't wake Hayden, Blaine padded barefoot to the living-room, looking for his phone. It lay on the coffee table, on top of the stack of magazines and newspapers Blaine had been reading the evening before in preparation for his show.

He stared at the words for a few seconds before pressing send. The phone went alive in his palm not a moment later, nearly flying off his hand as it vibrated, singing Queen's *Fat Bottomed Girls* – Blaine's personalised ringtone for Hayden.

"Hey," Blaine said when he picked up.

"Fucking finally," the voice on the other end said with an annoyed sigh. "Can't believe the bitch is out of our lives forever."

"Don't call her that."

"Trust me, hun, that's the nicest thing I've been calling her for quite some time."

Blaine could practically hear Hayden's eye roll. In his mind, he saw his best friend's lithe body folded in an arm chair, legs tucked underneath him, his bleached blond hair a tousled mess. Hayden worked non-stop when he was after a juicy article, and Blaine had no doubt he hadn't been to bed yet, whatever the time was in Boston.

"Things didn't work out, Hayden. It's nobody's fault."

Hayden scoffed. "Enough with the courteous bullshit, Blaine. We both know – hell, even she knows – that her lack of trust in you was what drove the marriage off the cliff. You never gave her any reason to doubt you and yet every time you left her sight she'd wonder if you were sucking some guy's dick."

"Hayden..." Blaine's voice was half plea, half warning. He didn't feel like rehashing the reasons behind his failed marriage anymore. He was tired of being the punching bag between his wife and his best friend.

"She hates me and you know it. She blames me, too. The bitch still thinks we start fucking the moment she turns her back on us."

"That's enough." The warning in Blaine's voice was hard to miss this time. Surprisingly, Hayden fell silent.

Blaine closed his eyes, his head falling back against the sofa. Behind his eyes, he could clearly see the hurt in Hayden's blue gaze – he'd seen it way too many times during the last few years when Blaine'd chosen Linda's side over his. Yet, Hayden had stubbornly refused to leave and had stuck by Blaine even when he'd had to swallow his pride.

"I'm tired, Hayden," he said when the silence stretched for too long. "It's over. The reasons why don't matter anymore. Can we just move past this?"

Hayden sighed. "Of course," he said softly, the tremor in his husky voice making Blaine's heart hurt.

"So, how's your article going? Did you find any evidence?"

The much needed change in topic made Hayden's voice brighten as he spoke about his investigation, the people he'd interviewed and what he'd found out. Blaine'd always been uncomfortable with the lengths Hayden would go to uncover the truth, always worrying that one day his best friend would get in too deep to claw his way back up. Hayden often brushed his concerns away with a wave of his hand, and a sarcastic remark that Blaine watched too many bad gangster films.

But this time, when Blaine asked him to be careful, Hayden paused before speaking.

"I'm being careful, babe. But this is too big to back away from." The quiet determination in Hayden's voice made Blaine's hackles rise.

"You come back here in one piece, you hear me? Don't go too far, Hayden." When Hayden didn't immediately reply, Blaine added, "Please."

“I won’t. I promise.”

Blaine wanted to believe him, but in his heart he knew Hayden had just made an empty promise.

Chapter two

Liam sat on a lonely bench in Hyde Park, tucked away from the main path and the horde of people milling around. The lovely April day seemed to have dragged everyone out of their offices to enjoy their lunch breaks in the sun, much like Liam. Weather in London was unpredictable, so people liked to take advantage of the sunshine any way they could.

The huge oak tree behind the bench cast a shadow over it, and Liam scooted closer to the edge where a nice sunny spot seemed unaffected by the wide tree branches. With a sigh, he opened his lunch box and studied the contents – a cream cheese and smoked salmon sandwich; some carrot sticks and a tiny hummus dip; a few green grapes. Usually, his mouth would start salivating at the sight of the food he'd prepared himself every morning, but today he wasn't feeling too enthusiastic about it.

Still, it was a shame to waste perfectly good food, so he grabbed a carrot and started munching on it, his mind drifting to the email he'd received this morning. No wonder he had no appetite after reading that.

His lying, cheating, son of a bitch ex-boyfriend had emailed him asking forgiveness, yet again. But what was worse, he'd threatened Liam that if he didn't reply to his numerous emails, texts, and calls, he'd come straight to the airport in a couple of weeks.

That threat had made Liam's blood boil. Not only was Jonathan a liar, a cheater, and a skilled manipulator, but he was a fucking arrogant bastard to even suggest he was still invited on that trip. Dropping the half-eaten carrot stick back in the lunch box, Liam took out his phone and opened his email app. He hadn't replied this morning because he'd been running late, and he'd learned the hard way to let himself cool down before saying or doing something out of spite.

But it'd been more than five hours since he'd first read the email. Plenty of time to cool down. Only, he hadn't. The anger still boiled in his gut and he wouldn't be able to think of anything else until he let Jonathan know exactly what he thought of his threats.

to: jonathan.f.reedjr@bt.com
from: liam_young@gmail.com

Jonathan,
I have nothing to say to you and I have no intention of answering any of your pathetic attempts to get in touch with me. I'm only replying to this email to let you know that if you have the audacity to show up at the airport, *uninvited*, I will cause the biggest scene Heathrow has ever witnessed.

Liam paused, his fingers hovering over the screen. Nothing could embarrass Jonathan more than public humiliation. Jonathan, with his posh accent and designer clothes and the cottage in the Cotswolds. Jonathan, whose parents would disown him if his name was ever mentioned in any sort of negative light.

God, Liam couldn't stand them. The only time he'd met them they'd treated him as if he was Jonathan's plaything, a temporary fixture in their lives that would soon be replaced with something more appropriate.

An idea struck him, his fingers flying over the letters.

Then, I'll blog about it, tweet about it, create a hundred fucking memes with your lying, cheating face on them, and make sure it all goes viral, and you get recognised everywhere you go.

There. That'd give Jonathan a pause before he decided to intrude on Liam's life any longer. What was more, Liam had no doubt Jonathan would believe every word and coward away, tail between his legs. Liam may only be a receptionist, for now, but he still worked for one of the biggest fashion magazines in Britain, *Flash*. He had the resources and the skills to make good on his threats.

His finger hovered over the send button, but Liam wondered if he should say anything else. He never wanted to talk to Jonathan ever again, so maybe it'd be wise to get it all off his chest before closing that chapter of his life for good.

I've been keeping silent and ignoring you because you're not worth my time, not anymore. Not after I wasted a year of my life with you only to find out you've been fucking anyone willing to spread their legs for you the whole time.
Do us both a favour and leave me alone. Plenty of dicks around for you to suck, why are you so obsessed with mine?
xoxo The One Who Got The Fuck Away

Liam read the email before sending it to make sure he hadn't mistyped a word. Satisfied with his spelling skills, he pressed send without hesitation. Something shifted inside him, making the tension in his body relax. He'd given himself a stiff neck and a headache, obsessing over Jonathan's email all morning. Now that it was dealt with, he could finally relax, enjoy his lunch and the nice, sunny day.

Only... This whole thing brought unpleasant memories to the front of his mind. Memories, he tried to ignore after every disappointment of a relationship he couldn't seem to stay away from. Liam Young, romance lover extraordinaire, always looking for love and always ending up getting hurt.

This pattern had to be broken. Liam didn't know how much more he could take before he lost his faith in love completely. From now on, he'd guard his heart, put up a tall, concrete fucking wall around it to protect it, and only give it to someone who truly deserved it.

Maybe not even then.

From now on, Liam would enjoy his single status and not rush into a relationship. He hadn't been single for more than a week since he was eighteen, it was time to break the serial dating habit and go for casual fun.

Digging into his sandwich with renewed fervour, Liam thought about the trip he'd booked over seven months ago. His dream holiday to Rio de Janeiro. He'd been saving for it for months and surprised Jonathan with it a week before he'd found him fucking some guy in a dark corner of a gay club, while he was supposedly on a work trip in Edinburgh.

God, such a waste! Liam'd spent days researching the best hotels, the safest neighbourhoods, the most enjoyable activities and day trips, only to have it all taken away. The trip was a package deal, and Liam had even managed to find a discount for couples without children. He couldn't go alone, he'd already pleaded his case with the travel agency, but they'd been adamant no changes could be made on the booking – both parties needed to be present in order for the reservation to be valid. The agent's whiny voice still rang in his ears as he remembered that particular, quite unpleasant, phone call.

If only he could find a Jonathan Reed in the next couple of weeks.

Chapter three

Blaine got out of the shower, tied a towel around his waist and wiped the bathroom mirror with his palm. After studying his reflexion for a few moments, he blew out most of the air in his lungs and shook his head. He looked tired, his blue eyes hooded with fatigue, dark circles dulling their usual sparkle. A shave seemed like a good idea, but he usually preferred the three day stubble covering his jaw to a clean shaven look.

Finishing in the bathroom, Blaine stepped out into his bedroom, turning on the digital radio he kept on his dresser. It was auto-tuned to RPRM FM, the radio station hosting Blaine's show, and he enjoyed listening to his colleagues' segments every day. The relatively new radio station was getting increasingly popular, especially among the younger generation. The eclectic mix of shows, indie music, talented DJs and fresh point of view on many current events turned RPRM FM into one of the most popular radio stations in Britain less than a year after it was launched. Blaine knew for a fact they had listeners overseas, too, taking advantage of the online live stream and podcasts, but the British twenty somethings were the radio's main audience.

The last notes of an upbeat pop song faded and Levi Stone's husky voice filled Blaine's bedroom as he rummaged through his underwear drawer looking for his favourite pair of Calvin Klein boxers. Today felt like a comfortable-yet-sexy-underwear kind of day.

"I've got a caller on the line," said Levi, the amusement in his voice making Blaine smile.

Levi's show was quite popular, his ratings shooting through the roof when he took people's calls. Blaine had his fair share of weird callers, but Levi attracted the crazy like no one else.

"And he's got something very interesting to say. Listen up, London, because at the end of this call you might be going to Rio de Janeiro. For free."

Blaine frowned. He wasn't aware of any games currently going on that offered a trip to Rio as the grand prize. Was he missing something here? He made a mental note to call his producer and ask, but first he was curious what Levi's caller had to say.

"Over to you, mate," Levi said, the static of the phone line crackling over the radio.

"Um, hi," the pleasant, soft voice sounded a bit off, as if he was outside and the connection wasn't very clear. "My name's Liam, and I'm looking for a Jonathan Reed to come on a luxury holiday to Rio de Janeiro with me."

Levi laughed before saying, "Will any Jonathan Reed do?"

"Pretty much. As long as he can take two weeks off at the end of May."

"I think you've got everyone very interested, Liam, but you'll need to elaborate a bit more than that."

Liam sighed heavily, pausing for a few seconds before speaking.

"I booked a couples holiday seven months ago but unfortunately my boyfriend and I split up, and I need someone to take his place, or I'll lose the holiday." He proceeded to explain how it was a package deal and he couldn't go alone. Levi asked a few questions to iron out the details, but Blaine barely heard any of it.

He wasn't a spiritual person, and he'd never believed in God or any sort of higher power. But in this moment Blaine felt like someone up there had finally taken pity on him and sent him an unexpected gift.

"I guess going on holiday with a complete stranger is a bit weird, yes," Liam was saying on the radio when Blaine focused his attention back on it. "But we don't have to stick together. We can do our own thing and basically just share a room in the hotel. It's actually a suite, so it's pretty big." Liam paused, and when he spoke again, emotion shook his voice. "I've always wanted to go to Rio. And I spent so much money on this trip and now it's all falling apart, and I'm out of ideas what to do."

"Did you hear that, folks? Help a guy out! Go with him to Rio!" Levi said, his cheerful voice in stark contrast with Liam's. He fired off the radio station's phone number and social media details, and urged people to help Liam find his Jonathan Reed.

When the next song on the playlist started, Blaine reached for his phone and dialled Levi's number.

"I need that kid's number," Blaine said when Levi picked up.

"Whoa, good to hear from you, too, mate," Levi drawled.

"I don't have time for pleasantries, Levi. The song will be over in three minutes and you'll be back on air, and I need the kid's number."

"I can't give it to you if you don't tell me why, man."

"You can but you're a nosy bastard who needs to know everything," Blaine said without any heat.

"Maybe." The smile in Levi's voice was infectious and Blaine felt his lips curving, too.

"My name's Jonathan Reed. Blaine is my middle name."

For once in his life Levi Stone was lost for words. "Seriously?" He finally asked.

"Yes. Now give me the number and pull the announcement off social media. Liam just found his Jonathan Reed."

A SIP OF RIO

Blaine was scrolling through his Twitter notifications when he heard the door opening, a burst of street traffic noise intruding on the calm serenity of the small coffee shop. Looking up from his phone, Blaine saw a guy dressed in ripped jeans and a black t-shirt that had *Queen* printed in large, pink letters at the front. When he turned slightly to close the door, Blaine's eyes landed on *Queen + Adam Lambert* tour dates listed on the back.

With a smile, and a small, amused shake of his head, Blaine raised an eyebrow, meeting the guy's eyes. He smiled, then rubbed the back of his neck before striding over to Blaine.

"Hi," he said, standing next to Blaine's table, his hands digging into his pockets. "I'm Liam?" He winced, probably regretting forming his introduction as a question.

Blaine bit his tongue, deciding against making a sarcastic comment. The guy seemed flustered enough, there was no need to torment him any more.

Plenty of time for that in Rio, Blaine thought with a smirk.

Standing up, Blaine offered his hand. "Nice to meet you, Liam. I'm Blaine Reed." Liam shook his hand tentatively, watching him with narrowed eyes. "Please take a seat."

Liam dragged the only other chair out from under the tiny table and sat, while Blaine caught the waitress' eye and nodded her over. After ordering a latte and a glass of water, Liam fidgeted in his seat, clearly uncomfortable.

He hadn't sounded that shy on the radio. He'd been a bit apprehensive when Blaine'd called, asking for them to meet, but Blaine never imagined the guy with the sexy, husky voice to be this young. He looked nineteen, twenty, tops. His unruly hair fell in waves past his ears, the curls the colour of caramel with the slightest hint of red. His skin was pale, freckles covering his nose. And his eyes... Blaine'd never seen eyes like Liam's. Thick dark lashes framed almond eyes the colour of smooth, light honey.

When Liam focused his gaze back on Blaine, he couldn't look away. The shy uncertainty in those magical eyes left Blaine speechless. A crease appeared between Liam's brows, and he licked his lips, raking a hand through his hair. The perfect Cupid's bow on those pink, kissable lips glistened with moisture, making Blaine's gut clench with lust.

"So," Liam said after clearing his throat. "You said on the phone that you know a Jonathan Reed?"

Liam's voice shook Blaine out of his increasingly inappropriate thoughts. He raised his coffee cup to his lips to buy himself a few moments before he spoke.

Did he really want to go on a romantic holiday with this guy? He'd met him five seconds ago and his dick was already getting hard for him. How would he resist when Liam pranced around in tight swimming trunks or, dear God, walked out of the bathroom wearing only a towel...

"Blaine?" Liam prompted, the crease between his brows deepening.

Why do I have to resist?

"I lied," Blaine finally said, and couldn't hold back his smirk when Liam's eyes narrowed.

"You lied?" He asked in disbelief.

"Yes. I don't know a Jonathan Reed." Blaine paused for effect, enjoying all too much the way Liam's nose wrinkled in distaste. He looked like he was a second away from losing his shyness completely and telling Blaine exactly where to stick it. "I *am* Jonathan Reed."

Liam's scowl deepened. "What?"

"Blaine's my middle name. Nobody's called me Jonathan since school. Nowadays my full name can only be found on legal documents and my passport." Blaine reached for his bag draped over the back of the chair. "Speaking of."

He dug around in the front pocket producing his passport and placing it on the table in front of Liam. Eying it suspiciously, Liam reached for it, opening it on the main page. His frown didn't ease as he studied Blaine's passport, but he managed a tight smile for the waitress who came back with his drinks.

When she departed, Liam gave Blaine his passport back, folding his arms. The look he was aiming at Blaine was somewhat wary, but a hint of amusement shone in his magical eyes.

"You have a flair for drama, don't you?" he said, eyebrow arching, lips curving into a smile.

"I'm afraid so."

They both laughed and just like that the ice was broken.

Chapter four

Liam's phone vibrated on top of the nightstand, waking him up. Uncharacteristically, he'd gone to bed before midnight, hoping to get a few extra hours sleep before the big staff meeting tomorrow. Usually, he hated staff meetings with passion, but he'd been looking forward to this one ever since he'd submitted his application for assistant photographer to HR last month.

Turning on his side, Liam stretched an arm out and grabbed his phone. He squinted at the screen when it lit up in the dark room, assaulting his bleary eyes. A selfie of Blaine wearing his radio headphones and a goofy smile on his face filled the screen, making Liam grin despite being woken up. He'd captioned it 'This time next week we'll be lying on a beach in Rio, baby!' followed by a thousand emojis of waves, cocktails, palm trees, and anything else even remotely holiday related Blaine could find.

Liam shook his head, his eyes raking over Blaine's wide blue eyes, always dancing with mischief, his infectious smile, his short, dark hair and sexy stubble. In the past week he and Blaine had been texting and talking every day, and become friends, of sorts. Liam ended up trusting Blaine too soon, as usual rushing head first into the new friendship. On several occasions, he'd had to remind himself to slow down, be more cautious, not reveal too much of himself too soon.

But resisting Blaine's charm was like trying to resist a hurricane. The guy was completely unaware of – or possibly ignoring – Liam's discomfort, and had managed to wrap him around his little finger in less than a week.

I was sleeping.

Liam sent his reply, the smile on his face refusing to disappear.

I bet my face was a good thing to wake up to, eh?

Liam rolled his eyes and started typing a response, but Blaine was faster, sending him a whole line of smirking emojis.

Do you have an emoji fetish or are you just verbally challenged?

Are you always so eloquent when just rolling out of bed?

I'm not rolling out of anything, I fully intend to ignore you and go back to sleep.

Cranky when woken up, noted. I'll try not to wake you up too much in Rio. I don't want to be kicked out of bed.

Liam snorted, fully awake now. His mind wandered to what it would be like to share a bed with Blaine. The moment he'd seen him in that coffee shop, all attitude and crystal blue eyes and swagger, Liam couldn't deny his immediate attraction. Unfortunately, crushing on a straight guy, especially a straight guy who'd shared he'd gotten through a nasty divorce, brought only heartbreak. Liam knew better. His self-preservation instinct was stronger now than when he was eighteen and treated like a dirty little secret by his best friend.

And yet the incurable romantic in him couldn't help but imagine what it would be like if Blaine was attracted to him, too. How it would feel to have Blaine's hands on his body, to feel Blaine's mouth on his skin...

No!

Liam chastised himself for going there, again, and typed his response.

I contacted the hotel asking for twin beds. Hopefully, they'll be on either side of the room so I won't hear you snore.

I don't snore!

Liam laughed when he received a whole lot of outraged emojis.

Good night, Blaine. Stop being useless and go do your job.

Blaine'd made it a habit to text Liam during his show once he found out Liam was a night owl like him. They usually ended up teasing each other, or jumping from topic to topic easily, or just being silly like tonight. The more Liam learned about Blaine, the more he liked him. His initial fear that going on holiday with a complete stranger would be awkward as fuck evaporated pretty fast, and he'd be lying to himself if he said he wasn't looking forward to two weeks alone with Blaine in Rio de Janeiro.

Liam frowned at the endearment, still not completely comfortable with Blaine calling him that, but unable to tell him to stop. He especially liked when Blaine said it out loud, his smooth voice making Liam's pulse quicken.

"You're such an idiot," Liam mumbled to himself, reaching to put the phone back on the nightstand.

It vibrated in his hand.

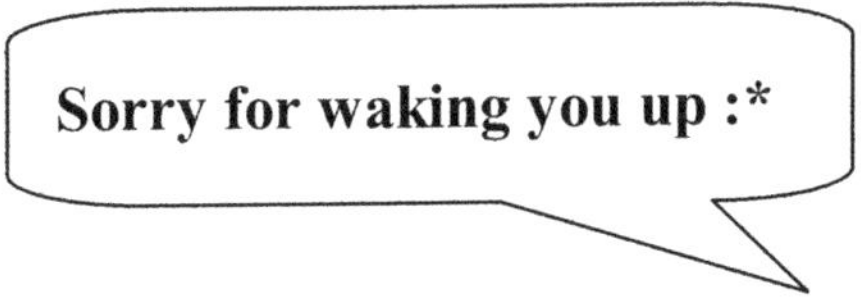

The kissing emoji in the end of the text made Liam's heart do a little flip inside his chest. He decided the best way to protect it was to ignore the message, *and* Blaine, for as long as he could.

Liam stormed out of the room the moment the staff meeting was dismissed. He didn't stop by the reception desk either, earning himself a curious look from Jenny, the other receptionist on duty today.

"Lunch," he threw over his shoulder, before pushing the heavy glass doors with more force than necessary, and bursting out of the building.

His hands shook when he took the sunglasses out of his bag. He needed a cigarette, but the disadvantage of being a non-smoker was that he never carried a pack with him.

So he did the next best thing. Taking his phone out of his pocket, Liam dialled Blaine's number.

"'ello?" Blaine's sleepy voice felt like a balm over Liam's injured ego.

"I didn't get the fucking job," Liam said. "They gave it to some slag from styling who doesn't even have a degree yet. I bet the skin tight dresses she always wears make up for the lack of qualification, though. After all, what's a degree compared to a slag in a short dress bending over to find the perfect angle for the shot? Over and over again."

Liam flopped down on an empty bench, his head already starting to pound with a massive headache.

"Whoa," Blaine exclaimed, sounding a bit more awake now. Liam heard the rustle of sheets through the phone, and then the opening and closing of doors. "Hang on, Sparky. I definitely need coffee to absorb that rant."

As if on cue Liam heard the unmistakable gurgle of the coffee maker coming to life.

"I'm so fucking sick of all this shit," Liam said, the fight draining out of him with a long sigh. "I'm tempted to just not go back there at all."

"I know how much you wanted this job, babe. You've been talking about it every day since we met. And it fucking sucks they gave it to the slag in the tight dress, but you know what? It's their loss. You are meant for something much better, much *bigger*, than an assistant photographer at a shitty fashion mag."

Blaine's voice had risen with every word as if he really believed what he was saying. Liam laughed humourlessly, leaning back on the bench and tilting his head towards the sky. It was gorgeously blue, a few fluffy white clouds sprinkled here and there, their shapes ever changing as they moved.

"Liam?"

"Sorry. I just..."

He just what? Liam couldn't put into words how he felt. He wanted to be mad, wanted the rejection to fuel his ambition to do better next time, to keep trying, keep sending out CVs and taking extra courses, and prove everyone who'd ever rejected him wrong.

But he just... Didn't care anymore.

"Look," Blaine said, his voice like a gentle caress on Liam's skin. "This time next week we'll be in Rio, enjoying ourselves, entirely oblivious to anything outside our perfect little holiday bubble. If you walk out on your job now, you won't be able to enjoy the dream holiday you fought so hard for." Blaine paused as if letting his words sink past Liam's disappointment. "You'll be worried about finding a new job the whole time."

Liam thought about it for a second, imagining going to Rio knowing he had no income to cover his rent, his bills pilling up, his savings running out. A shudder ran down his spine, followed by cold sweat despite the warm day.

"Yeah, I guess you're right," he admitted, throwing an arm over his eyes. "I can wait to fling my resignation letter in my boss' face and dramatically storm out of the building till we get back."

Blaine laughed, the sound already so familiar. A warm feeling cocooned Liam's rage, calming him and, in a way, giving him hope that things would work out eventually.

Maybe he really wasn't destined for this job after all, and something better was right around the corner.

"You'll have two whole weeks to plan your dramatic exit," Blaine said, the smile in his voice making Liam grin involuntarily too. "I took an ill-advised play writing course in college, I can help with all the planning."

"What did you study?" Liam asked, grateful for the change of topic. He was *tired* of agonising over his stupid job.

"Journalism and Mass Communication at the University of Westminster," Blaine said.

Liam grinned, irrationally happy that they had even more in common than he'd thought.

"I went for Media and Communication at Goldsmiths. Wanted to go for Photography, but my folks convinced me to do something with wider job prospects." Liam rolled his eyes even though Blaine couldn't see him. "Look at how well that turned out. I'm still waiting for my receptionist of the year award."

"Why did you take that job if it makes you so miserable?" Blaine asked without any accusation in his voice.

"Because I needed a job and that was the only one that paid enough to cover all my bills. I couldn't afford to do barely paid internships, not with rent prices in London." Liam exhaled loudly, remembering how scared he'd been when he couldn't find a decent job after months of sending CVs and going to interviews. "Besides, *Flash* is one of the best-selling fashion magazines in Britain. I thought it would be a nice stepping stone to bigger and better things." Liam felt his bad mood returning full force. "I guess I was wrong."

"Hey," Blaine said softly. "You're what? Twenty three? You have your whole life ahead of you. Just because you didn't get this job doesn't mean you won't get something better in the future."

"Twenty five."

"Really?" Blaine seemed genuinely amused.

"Yeah."

"When I first saw you I thought you were barely eighteen, with all those curls and freckles, and wide eyes."

Liam grinned. "I still get carded when I order a drink at the pub, so you're not alone."

Blaine chuckled, then Liam heard the distinct sound of a mug being placed on a glass table top.

"Sorry for waking you up, Blaine," Liam said, guilt settling over the disappointment and rage he'd felt a few moments ago. "I just needed to rant a little."

Liam could have called Becky or Stewart, but he knew how his friends would react – Becky would listen, exclaim in all the appropriate places, and then invite him over for pizza and cocktails while Stewart would probably find a way to make it all about himself in five minutes flat. He loved his two closest friends to death, but what he needed right now was Blaine's calm understanding.

How he'd come to *need* anything from Blaine in the short time he'd known the guy was something Liam wasn't willing to focus on at the moment.

"Any time."

They said their goodbyes and Liam tucked his phone back in his bag, pulling his sunglasscs over his eyes again. It was so tempting to say 'fuck it' and never go back behind that ultra modern glass and steel desk. But Blaine was right – in a week they'd be in Rio and Liam would enjoy his holiday much more if he didn't have to worry about job hunting.

What Liam absolutely intended to do right now was take a two hour lunch break. A small 'fuck you' of sorts. With a smile and newly-found spring in his step he headed to his favourite Italian restaurant, in his mind already picturing miles of golden sands, cold cocktails and hunky men in speedos playing football on the beach.

Chapter five

Blaine settled into his seat by the window and watched as Liam reached up to place his bag in the overhead locker. His t-shirt rode up revealing a sliver of white, hairless skin that Blaine ached to touch. Casting his eyes away, Blaine scolded himself for his thoughts yet again. Ever since he'd met Liam he couldn't get the guy out of his head. It was turning into a huge fucking problem. The last thing Blaine needed was jumping into a new relationship right after signing his divorce papers.

He'd been separated from Linda for nearly three years now, had even been with other people since then, but making it official had opened the wound and sprinkled a hefty dose of salt into it.

"Finally," Liam said as he collapsed in the seat next to him. "That was the longest queue for security ever. I thought we'd never make it to the plane in time." He started arranging his things in the pocket in front of him, dumping the blanket and tiny pillow at his feet.

They were travelling economy, but it was British Airways, so the seats were quite comfortable. Blaine was glad they'd managed to get two seats by the window instead of sharing with someone else in the middle four-seat aisle. The entertainment on board looked good, too, with lots of new films, TV shows, and music to keep them busy during the eleven hour flight.

After arranging everything to his liking, Liam leaned back into his seat and grinned at Blaine.

"Nearly there," he said with a dreamy sigh.

"You never told me, why Rio?" Blaine asked, relaxing back into his own seat, turning to face Liam.

"Hm?" Liam frowned.

"Your dream destination. It could have been some exotic island or a romantic cabin in the Alps or a glamorous cruise. Why Rio?"

Liam blushed a little. "My aunt Annie – she's great, my favourite person in the world." He grinned widely, as if he couldn't help it. His beautiful honey eyes softened with affection as he kept talking. "When I was little, she used to look after me when Mum had to go back to work, so I got to spend a lot of time with her when I was a kid. Then, when I grew older, I'd stay with her for the weekend, just to hang out. She'd take me travelling with her sometimes. She loves travelling – she's been everywhere! As soon as she got her royalty check she'd start planning her next trip."

Liam's unfocused gaze drifted away as if remembering all the good times he'd had with his aunt. His grin slipped a little and he licked his lips, his eyes moving past Blaine to look outside the window.

"What does she do?" Blaine asked softly, trying to coax Liam back to the story.

"She's a writer."

"Yeah?" Blaine asked with a smile. "What does she write?"

Liam chuckled before replying. "Historical horror novels."

"That sounds... interesting."

"It is. Her novels are fun and quirky, and she has a loyal fan base. She's been doing it for twenty years now."

"I'm not really into horror, but I may have seen her books in the bookshop. What's her full name?"

"She writes under Hazel Rogers," Liam said, then listed some of his aunt's more popular titles. Turned out Blaine hadn't read or heard of any of them but made a mental note to check them out.

"So, anyway," Liam waved a hand, the elegant gesture helping him get back on track. "The first time she went to Rio – I think I was around seventeen – she came back in tears. Scared the hell out of my mum when we met her at the airport. Turned out Aunt Annie was crying because she didn't want to leave Rio. She'd fallen in love with the city and seemed to have left her heart there." Liam rolled his eyes making Blaine grin despite the sad part in the story. "Aunt Annie has a way with words. She talks like that all the time as if it's completely normal."

Blaine heard the doors of the plane close, flight attendants walking up and down the aisles, closing the overhead compartments and making sure everyone'd fastened their seatbelts.

"She talked about Rio all the time to a point we all felt like we'd been there ourselves. When Dad mentioned that to her she was outraged and said," Liam paused, schooling his features and doing an impression of his aunt's voice. "Graham, you can't experience Rio through someone's stories or a television program, or even a book. You need to *immerse* yourself in its atmosphere, in its very core, and trust me when I say this – once you do you may never want to leave."

Blaine had to smile at Liam's bad voice impression. "I'm pretty sure your aunt doesn't sound like an eighty-year-old spinster from the 1920s."

Liam smacked him on the upper arm, ignoring his comment. "Her eyes watered when she said that, even though she'd been home for months. Mum suspected she'd met someone there, unable to believe her sister had actually fallen in love with a *place*." Liam shook his head, running a hand through his hair. "So anyway, Aunt Annie started saving for her next trip to Rio the moment she came back. But eight months later she was diagnosed with a heart condition and strict orders to avoid flying at all costs."

Blaine's heart sank. "So she never went back?"

Liam's curls moved, catching the light in their brown depths as he shook his head. He seemed so sad. Blaine wanted to wrap an arm around his shoulders and bury his fingers in that silky hair, offering silent support.

Of course, he didn't.

"No, she didn't."

The flight attendant requested everyone's attention for the safety briefing as the plane taxied out of the bay. Nobody paid any attention to the poor guy demonstrating how the oxygen masks and life jackets worked.

"We planned to go together before she was diagnosed," Liam continued, lowering his voice. "And after," he swallowed with difficulty, biting his lip. "I promised her I'd go anyway."

"Was she excited when you finally booked the trip?"

"Yeah," Liam said with a sad smile. "She always said I should go with someone special the first time. I thought Jonathan was that someone."

"I'm sorry," Blaine said, bumping his shoulder to Liam's.

Liam waved a hand, dismissing Blaine's concern, his brilliant smile reaching his eyes again. "Forget about all this, alright? We're going to have an amazing time!" Blaine nodded, meeting Liam's eyes and then unable to look away. "No more talk about cheating boyfriends, disease or broken dreams. We're officially entering the holiday bubble."

Blaine laughed, earning himself a glare from the flight attendant who was gesturing towards the emergency exits enthusiastically.

"What's in your bubble?" Blaine asked, lowering his voice once again. He was pretty sure the guy was going to spit in his food later.

"Cocktails, music, sand, waves, and hot men running around in speedos," Liam said with relish.

"And sunscreen," Blaine added, his gaze pointedly drifting to the freckles around Liam's nose.

"Oh, and photos! I plan on taking a ton of pictures." Liam's eyes narrowed as they slid down Blaine's body. "You should pose for me."

Blaine laughed again, couldn't help it. Thankfully, the flight attendant had finished his presentation and was nowhere to be seen. The plane had stopped moving, probably being held in line for access to the runway.

"Me? I'm a radio DJ, not a model."

"Aww, come on, Blaine," Liam cooed, his finger coming to trace Blaine's cheekbone. "I can totally see it: sunset at Copacabana, you propped on your elbows on the shore, head thrown back as the waves lap at your feet..."

Blaine snorted loudly, interrupting Liam's vision.

"You're an asshole, you know that?" Liam said, leaning back in his seat and closing his eyes as the plane started moving again.

“I’ve been told once or twice.” Blaine studied Liam’s profile, taking the opportunity to stare at him undisturbed while Liam couldn't see him. “Why did you decide to go in May? Most people go for the carnival or for Christmas.”

Liam exhaled loudly before opening his eyes to look at Blaine.

“It’s my birthday in May,” he said sheepishly.

“What? When?” Blaine exclaimed, feeling unprepared. If he’d known sooner he’d have come up with a thoughtful present or some sort of birthday surprise.

“I’m not telling you,” Liam said, taking the little pillow he’d dropped to the floor and putting it behind his head. Leaning back on it, he closed his eyes again, and ignored Blaine’s frown.

Blaine snatched the pillow from behind Liam’s head with one swift motion, fully enjoying Liam’s squeak as he bumped his head on the headrest.

“I’m going to find out,” Blaine said, tucking the pillow behind his own head and settling comfortably.

“It’s going to be a long flight,” Liam murmured just as the airplane’s powerful engines came to life and they accelerated down the runway.

A SIP OF RIO

Even at eleven o'clock at night, the humid heat in Rio de Janeiro was unbearable. Blaine didn't even want to think about what it would be like under the scorching sun the next day.

"I thought May was one of the coolest months in Rio," Blaine said with a sideways glance at Liam who was pulling his suitcase next to him, looking around for any signs of their pre-booked taxi service.

"It is. This is what 'cool' means in Rio."

Blaine groaned, pulling to a stop in front of the taxi stand.

"You'll feel much better at the beach tomorrow, with cocktail in hand and the breeze from the sea," Liam offered with a wink, before he started waving frantically at something. "It's our taxi," he threw over his shoulder, and took off towards a black Ford.

The ride to their hotel was shorter than Blaine expected. Rio was beautiful at night, the lights from the tiny houses in the *favelas* on the hills spread across the whole city, twinkling like fireflies in the night. The statue of Christ the Redeemer was lit up in green light and could be seen through their entire journey. There was something in the air... something Blaine couldn't explain. Maybe Liam's aunt had been right – maybe there was some sort of magic at work in Rio de Janeiro.

Liam's face was glued to the window the entire ride to the hotel. His eyes wide with wonder, and his lips curved into a blissful smile, he reminded Blaine of a manga character, all big eyes, alabaster skin, and elegant fingers.

"Do you feel it?" Liam whispered without turning to face Blaine as if afraid he might miss something worth seeing outside.

"Feel what?"

"The magic."

Blaine closed his eyes for a moment, his finger tips burning with the need to touch some physical manifestation of what he was already feeling in his gut.

"Yeah," he whispered back, wishing it was jetlag, and tomorrow he'd feel normal again.

"Me too," Liam said with a deep, content sigh.

When the car pulled up in front of their hotel, Blaine gasped in surprise. He'd never asked Liam about details – it was a free holiday, after all. They could have stayed at a run-down motel and he still wouldn't have cared as long as it was clean and safe. He'd never expected to be staying at a five-star hotel right at the beach front.

Hotel Fasano had an elegant, understated quality to it that Blaine immediately liked. There were no golden chandeliers or marble floors, or, God forbid, bronze statues. Way too many hotels these days tried to push their opulence in your face, to a point where it became too kitschy for Blaine's taste.

With the corner of his eye Blaine saw Liam give the driver a tip, then lug both their suitcases towards the hotel entrance.

"Sorry..." Blaine began, all too aware he'd been staring at the hotel and the gorgeous beach right across the road, completely forgetting about everything else.

"No worries. Here," Liam passed him the suitcase handle and they walked inside the hotel lobby.

A cheerful receptionist greeted them from behind a huge wooden desk. After checking their IDs, she confirmed the reservation and proceeded to list all the facilities they could take full advantage of during their stay – the rooftop pool; sauna, gym, and spa centre; award winning Italian restaurant; twenty-four-hour room service. Blaine spaced out at some point, too tired to even summon the energy to look interested.

"Thank you," Liam's polite, but firm voice caught Blaine's attention. "But if you don't mind, we'd like to go up to our room. We just landed after an eleven hour flight and we're exhausted."

"Of course!" The woman exclaimed and handed Liam their key cards. "Oh," she added as they stepped away from the desk. "I can see my manager left a note on your reservation – you requested a suite with twin beds instead of a double last week?" Liam nodded. "I'm sorry Mr Young, but all our suites come with double beds, so we couldn't accommodate your request."

"Shit," Liam murmured softly, running a hand through his hair and glancing at Blaine. "Can we at least get an extra bed in?"

The poor receptionist looked confused, a small crease appearing between her eyebrows as her eyes moved from Liam to Blaine.

Oh, for fuck's sake.

"It's fine, don't worry about it," Blaine said to her, then added softly for only Liam to hear, "I don't mind sleeping in the same bed, plenty of room. Let's just go before I pass out right here."

Liam looked like he wanted to argue, but instead he nodded slowly, exhaustion etched on his face.

"Are you sure?" Liam asked when the elevator doors closed behind them.

"Positive."

"We can ask them for an extra bed tomorrow when we're rested and not so desperate for *any* bed..."

Blaine flicked a look in Liam's direction to find him worrying his plump lower lip as if to stop himself from saying anything else.

"If you really want to sleep in a fold out bed, be my guest. I'm keeping the double bed."

Liam smiled, biting the inside of his cheek as he nodded.

The elevator dinged, announcing their arrival on the fifth floor. Rolling their suitcases to their room, Blaine nearly moaned with relief once Liam unlocked the door and held it for him.

"One step closer to getting some sleep. I think I've been awake for nearly twenty-four..." Blaine's words died on his tongue as the lights in the room came to life. "Hours," he managed to say before turning to Liam. "My God, this must have cost you a fortune."

The suite was impressive. Floor to ceiling windows took up one whole wall, leading to a softly lit terrace with a table, set of chairs tucked underneath and what looked like a hammock on the other side.

On his right, an elegant voile curtain separated the bedroom from the sitting area on his left. A plush white sofa and a dark wood coffee table were arranged in front of a huge flat screen TV in the lounge, while the king size bed on the other side of the curtain drew Blaine in like a siren song. His shoes clacked on the hardwood floor as he made his way to the bed and fell on it face first.

"God, this feels good," he said with a loud groan muffled by the comforter.

Liam chuckled somewhere behind him before the mattress dipped when he sat on the other side of the bed.

"At least take your clothes off and brush your teeth before you pass out," he said, followed by the distinct thump of shoes hitting the floor.

"Yessir," Blaine mumbled, his words already slurring together.

He could do this. He could stay awake for five more minutes to undress and brush his teeth. He totally could, but the bed felt so good, so soft...

"Blaine!"

"I'm going, I'm going!" Blaine swayed on his feet a little as Liam's voice startled him. "Bossy bastard."

It might have been his imagination, but Blaine thought he heard Liam's husky laughter following him to the bathroom.

A few minutes later, they were both undressed and somewhat clean under the blanket. The air conditioning hummed softly in the background and the only light in the room came from the soft lamps outside on the terrace. They lay on their sides facing each other, their blinks getting longer and longer until exhaustion took over and sleep claimed them.

Chapter six

Awareness nudged at Liam's consciousness, pulling him out of his dreamless slumber. Squinting one eye open, he was instantly blinded by the sunshine filtering in the room from the huge windows. For a second or two he had no idea where he was, but then reality slammed into his brain.

Rio.

A smile pulled at his lips, his body protesting as he tried to stretch. Liam's tired limbs weren't the only thing stopping him from changing his position. A solid, warm body was plastered to his back, an arm draped around Liam's waist.

"Shit," Liam murmured, trying to dislodge Blaine and get up.

Blaine grunted when Liam tried to slip free of his embrace, pulling him even closer. Liam's ass came to rest right against Blaine's groin, the rigid length of his cock hard to ignore. Heat pooled in Liam's belly, the instinct to grind against Blaine too strong to resist.

No. He wasn't doing this. Not here, not now, not when he was finally in Rio and dead set on enjoying every moment of the next two weeks. Agonising over his crush on a straight guy was not the way he intended to spend his dream holiday.

"Get off me," he said, pushing Blaine's arm off his waist, then sitting up. "Fuck," he murmured, burying his face in his hands when his bare feet touched the floor.

It was only morning wood. Biology. Human nature. Nothing more, nothing less.

It did *not* mean Blaine was in any way attracted to him. Yeah, the guy was a bit more touchy-feely than most straight men Liam knew, but that didn't mean anything. His dad had probably given him enough hugs as a child and hadn't imprinted any macho bullshit on his brain, that was all.

"And here I was thinking Rio would bring out your sunny personality," Blaine said softly.

Liam turned to look at him over his shoulder, scowling. He opened his mouth to tell Blaine they were definitely asking for an extra bed today, but no words came out. Blaine was lying on his side, the shape of Liam's body still evident on the sheets in front of him. His eyes were closed, but a tiny, devilish smile played on his lips. The white sheet pooled around Blaine's waist, revealing the smooth skin on his arms and the light dusting of dark hair on his chest.

"When you said there's plenty of room for both of us on the bed I didn't imagine we'd sleep pressed together in the middle." Liam's words were clipped, his eyes still glued to Blaine's body.

"What can I say," Blaine drawled, his eyelids lifting a little to reveal twinkling blue eyes. "I'm a cuddler."

"You're incorrigible, that's what you are," Liam said with a loud huff, moving to stand up.

"You love it," Blaine said, stretching on the bed, then tucking his hands behind his head.

Liam flicked a glance at him and all thoughts of extra beds vanished. The guy was gorgeous and Liam was only human. This whole thing would end up in disaster but he couldn't find it in himself to put any kind of distance between them.

As if reading his thoughts, Blaine smirked, his gaze never straying from Liam's. The sheet had slid lower when he'd moved, revealing black ink on the side of his stomach. Liam frowned, trying to see what it was, but the angle wasn't right and he could only see part of it.

"It's a baby dragon," Blaine said, his voice claiming Liam's attention.

Liam felt his cheeks burn when he refocused his eyes on Blaine's. Pushing back the instinct to apologise for shamelessly ogling his body, Liam willed his traitorous blush to subside, then asked,

"What does it mean?"

He thought it was odd that Blaine'd specified it was a *baby* dragon, as if that particular characteristic meant something.

"It means that however big or strong or powerful you're meant to be, you still have to hatch first."

Liam nodded with a slight frown, unsure of the exact meaning behind Blaine's words, but already feeling like the moment had stretched for too long.

"Right," he said, putting his hands on his hips and trying to focus. "I'm going to call Reception and ask for an extra bed." Blaine gave him a searching look, but before he could open his mouth to say anything, Liam continued. "I'm not comfortable sleeping like this." He waved his hand in Blaine's direction, trying to indicate their cuddling moment with a swift motion of his hand.

Blaine sighed, pulling the sheet up to his chest before sitting on the bed.

"I'm sorry," he said earnestly, all trace of mischief gone from his tone. "It's true, though – I *am* a cuddler. But," he raised a hand to silence Liam's protest. "I was really tired last night. I don't even remember falling asleep or even moving during the whole night. I promise I'll behave from now on and keep to my side of the bed."

Liam studied him, crossing his arms over his chest. Blaine sounded sincere, but was that enough? Could he withstand the torture of sleeping in the same bed with a gorgeous guy every night for two weeks when he knew nothing could happen between them?

"Look." Blaine planted his feet on the floor and stood up, the sheet falling back on the mattress. His white boxers left little to the imagination and Liam struggled with the effort to keep his eyes firmly on Blaine's face. "The last thing I want to do is ruin this trip for you. If it makes you that uncomfortable, we'll get the extra bed and I'll sleep in it, okay?" Blaine walked closer, placing his palms on Liam's shoulders. "But I promise you I'll behave."

Liam found it hard not to believe the sincerity in Blaine's earnest blue eyes. In his mind, a whirlwind of emotions was confusing the fuck out of him.

"Hey," Blaine said softly. "I don't think I ever said thank you."

"For what?"

"Letting me tag along on your dream holiday." Blaine winked, then turned on his heel and headed for the bathroom.

Despite the conscious effort not to look, Liam's eyes slid down Blaine's broad back to the round globes of his ass covered in thin, white cotton. When Blaine closed the door behind him, Liam shook his head, thinking he'd be lucky if he left Rio with his heart intact.

Still a little jet-lagged even after a full night's sleep, Liam couldn't be bothered to even open his notebook where he'd jotted down notes about all the things he wanted to do in Rio. Armed with towels, sun screen, and a couple of paperbacks, he and Blaine crossed the road that separated their hotel and Ipanema beach. The weather was beautiful – the breeze from the ocean lifting the otherwise oppressive humid heat and creating playful waves that crashed on the shore, creating the perfect soundtrack of the day.

Near Posto 8, a large rainbow flag was proudly waving in the wind, marking *Farme Gay* beach – a part of Ipanema between Posto 8 and Posto 9, a favourite daytime meeting place of Rio's LGBT community. Rainbow flags could be seen on every street vendor, food stall and bar nearby, and many gay couples chose that part of the beach to lounge and sunbathe without having to worry about being judged.

"Fuck, this is perfect," Blaine said with a long, content sigh as he lay on top of the beach towel.

This close Liam could inspect the tattoo on Blaine's hip without being too obvious about it. Part of the ink was still concealed under Blaine's trunks, but Liam could clearly see the baby dragon, hatching from the egg, fierce despite its size. The artistry behind the tattoo was incredible. Liam marvelled at the vivid colours and masterful shadows making the dragon so lifelike it seemed to come to life with every move Blaine made.

"You should really put some sun screen on that pale skin of yours," Blaine said, jerking Liam out of his thoughts.

"What about you? You're like *one* shade darker than me, which still puts you in the baby powder category."

Liam pulled the bag closer to him, rummaging through it to locate the bottle of sun screen.

Blaine snorted. "True. But I tan easily. You, on the other hand, don't."

"How do you know that?" Liam uncapped the bottle and squeezed some lotion on his palm, rubbing it into his legs.

"I can tell," Blaine said, lifting one shoulder elegantly. "Your skin's kinda pink. And you have freckles."

Blaine traced a patch of freckles on Liam's shoulder with the tip of his finger. Liam started, his hands faltering as he was spreading the sun screen on his body. Blaine dropped his hand, then tucked it underneath his head, pushing the sunglasses up on his head.

"Do you need help with your back?" Blaine's intense blue stare stole Liam's breath. He'd give anything to have Blaine's hands on him, but an insistent voice in his head kept screaming at him to back away.

Run.

Liam ignored it.

"Sure," he said, passing Blaine the bottle.

How could he listen to the voice? He'd become friends with Blaine even before they'd boarded the plane, and he hoped they would keep in touch once they got back to London. Even if friends is not what he wanted them to be.

"God, your shoulders are stiff," Blaine said, massaging a generous amount of lotion into Liam's skin. "You have knots the size of golf balls."

Blaine rubbed Liam's skin, squeezing gently then massaging the sore spot. Liam could feel his muscles relaxing under Blaine's touch and he had to bite his lip to stop the moan threatening to escape.

"All done," Blaine said, passing Liam the bottle.

Liam mumbled his thanks, then concentrated on trying to calm down his raging hard on. Blaine's touch made need coil in the pit of Liam's stomach, even if it was entirely platonic on his friend's side.

Pulling his knees to his chest, Liam stared into the ocean, emptying his mind of everything else but the rolling waves. The smell of salt water. The gentle caress of the breeze. The faint music that could be heard from the beach bar nearby. The voices and soft laughter of people around them.

"Liam? You alright, babe?" Blaine asked, startling him out of his trance.

The soft pressure of Blaine's hand on his lower back sent shock waves of desire and confusion straight to his gut, making Liam jump. He had to put some distance between them before he spontaneously combusted.

"I'm going to get us something to drink," he said, hastily, not meeting Blaine's eyes. "What do you want?"

Blaine's eyebrows furrowed over the top of his sunglasses but he didn't comment on Liam's neurotic behaviour. He asked for a green coconut and Liam all but ran toward the bar on the other side of the beach.

He ordered two coconuts for both of them, watching in fascination as the guy behind the counter skilfully cut the coconuts' tops off without spilling a drop of liquid. He then stuck straws inside the fruit, and colourful cocktail umbrellas, before handing Liam the drinks.

"*Obrigado*," Liam said, using one of the few words he knew in Portuguese. The guy smiled crookedly and saluted Liam before he walked away, hands full with the two large coconuts.

"Mmmm, that's delicious," Blaine said after taking a sip of the coconut's juice.

Liam nodded, taking a seat beside him on the beach towel and trying his own drink. He'd had coconut milk before but the green coconut juice was an entirely different thing. It tasted sweet, but it was refreshing without overwhelming the senses. The perfect drink for a hot day on the beach.

The rest of the afternoon passed quickly. As if catching on to Liam's discomfort, Blaine distanced himself a little, the subtle changes in his behaviour impossible to ignore. During lunch at the cosy cafe nearby, Blaine sat opposite Liam instead of next to him, and seemed distracted even if he conversed effortlessly. Later, when they settled back on the beach for a couple of hours, Blaine pulled the sunglasses over his eyes and fell asleep, snoring softly.

In that moment, even sitting right next to him, Liam missed him. Blaine's affectionate personality made it harder to ignore the butterflies in his gut every time he touched him, but once Blaine's attention was taken away, Liam felt its absence like a missing limb.

With a shake of his head, Liam refused to let his mind wander any deeper into these thoughts. After covering Blaine's body with his t-shirt and his face with a hat so that he didn't burn to a crisp as he slept, Liam dug a paperback out of the bag, settled comfortably on his belly, and started reading. It was the first book in a fantasy series he'd been meaning to read for a while, a fast-paced whirlwind of mysterious worlds, magical creatures, and dragons. Yeah, dragons would do.

"So, what do you wanna do tonight?"

Liam turned, a little startled by Blaine's voice. He hadn't heard the man open the bathroom door and walk out while he'd been staring out the window, deep in thought.

"I'm not..." Liam turned, facing Blaine and his brain short circuited. "Sure," he managed to finish his sentence, his eyes roaming over the body of the man less than a foot away from him.

Blaine was still wet from the shower, droplets of water running down his naked chest, a white towel tied loosely around his hips. Liam'd seen him in trunks today, it wasn't like he was seeing Blaine's body for the first time. And yet the sight of his flushed, damp skin made Liam's mouth water. They were standing so close that Liam could feel the heat coming off Blaine's skin, smell the fruity scent of his shampoo.

"Liam?"

"Um, yes. Tonight." Liam took a hasty step back, glancing away from the gorgeous man in front of him. "I don't know. What do you want to do?" He busied himself with gathering the toiletries he'd need in the shower.

"Let's go grab some dinner and then maybe a couple of drinks? I can check out the local bars and restaurants online while you shower."

"Sounds good," Liam threw over his shoulder before slamming the bathroom door behind him.

Resting his head back against the door, Liam closed his eyes and tried to focus. He was acting like an idiot, lusting after his friend and possibly ruining this holiday for both of them. Blaine hadn't been anything but supportive, helpful and easy-going, and just as excited as Liam about this trip.

He needed to get his shit together before things got awkward between them.

Liam relaxed back in his chair, looking around the restaurant, hoping to catch the eye of their waiter and order another glass of wine. The food had been amazing and the chilled white wine's fruity undertones complemented the delicious meal perfectly. He could have another glass with dessert. Besides, neither him nor Blaine were in a hurry to leave yet. The vibrant, air-conditioned restaurant was a godsend after spending the entire day outside in the humid heat.

Blaine brushed his knee alongside Liam's under the table, claiming his attention.

"You OK?" He asked, and there was that brush of skin again. Liam squirmed in his chair, sitting upright, severing any unsolicited contact.

"Yeah. Just looking for the waiter." Liam's eyes scanned the restaurant again, the perfect excuse to glance away from Blaine's searching gaze. "I'm going to get another glass of wine and the caramel sundae for dessert. What would you like?"

Finally, Liam spotted their waiter and beckoned him over with a smile and a wave of his hand. The guy smiled back and strutted towards them, his eyes meeting Liam's briefly before settling on Blaine. Just as they had every time since they'd been shown to their table.

Liam rolled his eyes before meeting Blaine's gaze again, fighting the instinct to scowl. Blaine was watching him, his full attention focused on Liam even when the waiter arrived at their table.

"You ready for dessert, guys?" The waiter crooned in his accented English, standing so close to Blaine that his hip nearly rested on Blaine's upper arm.

His good mood quickly evaporating, Liam couldn't help the terse tone when he spoke.

"Yes. Another glass of wine and the caramel sundae for me, please." He arched an eyebrow at Blaine, remembering he hadn't said if he wanted anything for dessert.

He can order his own fucking dessert. Waiter boy was drooling all over him anyway.

"I'll have the same. Thanks," Blaine said politely, but the dismissal in his voice was evident.

"You've got it," the waiter said with a disappointed pout, and left.

"What's wrong?" Blaine asked, taking a sip of his wine before leaving the empty glass on the table.

Liam didn't want to do this right now. This holiday was turning out to be nothing like he'd imagined. Everything was falling apart in his mind, the confusing feelings he had for Blaine squeezing like a tight band around his heart, not letting him enjoy the trip he'd been dreaming about for years.

But what could he say? Blaine hadn't done anything wrong. It wasn't his fault Liam had developed feelings for the man – purely physical, lustful feelings – and it wasn't like Liam could voice his troubles, was it? If he had any chance to salvage this holiday he needed to get over himself, relax and stop obsessing over something he couldn't have.

Blaine's heavy sigh brought Liam out of his thoughts and he realised with horror he hadn't said anything in a few minutes, or answered Blaine's question.

"If you're done scowling at your empty glass, could you maybe voice some of those thoughts?" Blaine folded his arms and leaned back in his chair, feigning nonchalance but Liam knew better. The crease between Blaine's eyes was a dead giveaway he was worried. "I can't read minds, you know?" Blaine winked at him, but the worry in his eyes remained.

"I'm sorry," Liam said, schooling his features into what he hoped was a relaxed expression. "I'm fine."

Blaine raised an eyebrow.

"I'm a little overwhelmed, I guess," Liam continued when he saw Blaine wasn't going to let this go. "I've been dreaming of this for so long and we're finally here, but..." He paused, wondering how to be somewhat honest but not offend or mislead Blaine.

"But you're here with me instead of your boyfriend, and you miss him and you're starting to regret this whole thing." Blaine's face distorted into a disappointed frown, the hurt evident in his eyes.

Liam's eyes widened. "No!" He exclaimed, a bit louder than he meant to. "I don't miss *him*," he said, his voice lower. A quick scan of the tables around them proved that nobody was paying them any attention, so he continued. "I'm glad you're here with me." Blaine held Liam's eyes, searching for the truth behind that statement. His fiery blue gaze softened as he nodded.

"It's just a little different than what I imagined but that doesn't mean it's not great," Liam continued. "Like I said, I'm just a little overwhelmed, but I'll be fine. We've been here a day, I need some time to relax and leave London behind."

"Okay," Blaine said, his full lips curving into a smile.

God, there was so much mischief behind that smile.

Just as Liam was about to lose all control, drag Blaine over the table and kiss the fuck out of him, waiter boy appeared all flustered and panting as if he'd run around the restaurant a few dozen times. Again, he acknowledged Liam, but had eyes – and flirty smiles – only for Blaine.

"Sorry about the wait, guys," he purred, as he placed the sundaes and glasses of wine in front of them. "It's crazy in here today," he added with an expressive eye roll. "How long are you guys in town for? I don't think I've seen you here before." His eyes roamed over Blaine shamelessly. "I'd remember," he added with a wink.

The urge to pour the cold glass of wine on his head grew inside Liam with every passing second.

"We just arrived yesterday," Blaine said politely. "We're staying for a couple of weeks."

"Ahh, *entendo*! How do you like Rio so far?" He placed a hand on Blaine's shoulder and Liam couldn't take it anymore.

"We like it fine!" He snapped.

Both waiter boy and Blaine startled, looking at him as if he'd lost his mind. Well, the waiter was. Blaine's eyes held as much mirth as surprise.

"Well..." the waiter drawled, rolling his eyes at Blaine. He ignored him, biting his lips against a smile, but his eyes never left Liam's. "Enjoy your dessert," he said tersely, aiming a glare in Liam's direction before – finally – departing.

"If looks could kill..." Blaine said, plunging his spoon deep into the sundae and scooping an obscene amount of ice cream into his mouth.

Liam felt embarrassment creep up his neck, reddening his cheeks. He wasn't in the habit of acting like a jealous teenager, but there was something really annoying about that guy. He couldn't stand the overly familiar way he acted with Blaine as if he had the right. As if he was the one who'd woken up with Blaine's hard on nestled against his ass.

The moment the thought crossed his mind, Liam realised he was making a claim on Blaine, even if it was only in his own head, and he had no right to do that.

Fucking hell he needed another drink, a much stronger one.

"I've no idea what's going on in your head, babe," Blaine said, sitting back after finishing half of his sundae in record time, while Liam's was starting to melt, untouched. Irritated, Liam stabbed his spoon in it and brought it to his mouth, the ice cream and the generous helping of caramel sauce melting on his tongue.

"Oh my God," he exclaimed, his mouth still full of ice cream. "Do you think he spit in my sundae?"

Blaine burst out laughing, the melodic sound so uninhibited and free it gave Liam goosebumps. The man was gorgeous in any shape or form, but when he laughed, Liam's world stopped turning.

"I guess we'll never know," Blaine said, his grin still firmly in place. His eyes sparkled from laughing, and probably from the several glasses of wine, and he was ridiculously beautiful.

"That's not what you say when someone asks you if someone spit in their food!" Liam said in mock outrage.

"No, dear, I'm sure the nice waiter twink didn't spit in your sundae, dear," Blaine said, placing his elbows on the table and resting his chin on his hands.

"Now, see? That's more like it." Liam scooped another generous helping of ice cream, his gaze locked on Blaine's.

"So, I was about to say before the thorn in your side appeared, that..."

"He's not a thorn in my side!" Liam protested.

"That," Blaine said pointedly, ignoring Liam's comment. "I found a really nice bar close by, if you want to let loose a little, have a few drinks."

In all honesty, Liam wanted to have more than a few drinks. He wanted to dance, to feel someone's hands all over him, to make out with a hot guy and try to get all thoughts of Blaine out of his head.

However, he doubted the kind of bar he was thinking about was the kind of bar Blaine was referring to.

"It's a gay bar, Liam," Blaine said, as if reading Liam's mind. How did he do that? "See? I'm getting better at reading you."

Liam wanted to scowl but the huge smile Blaine aimed his way disarmed him of any irritation.

"You don't mind going to a gay bar?"

"Why would I? A bar is a bar."

Liam quirked an eyebrow, countless examples of how a gay bar was nothing like a straight bar on the tip of his tongue.

"It's not like I've never been to a gay bar, Liam. Relax before you get an ulcer." Blaine caught the waiter's eye, much faster than Liam had before, and signalled for the bill.

He'd been to a gay bar? Why? Was it just as a wing man for someone? Or with other friends and colleagues?

Or... But it couldn't be, could it? Blaine wasn't gay. It would explain a lot about his behaviour, and God knows Liam's prayers would be answered, but he'd been married. To a woman, for fuck's sake.

Was he bi? Curious? Enjoyed a good time with a guy once in a while but otherwise pretended to be straight?

And why the fuck hadn't he said anything to Liam until now?

"Liam?" The softness in Blaine's voice was mirrored in his eyes when Liam looked at him. Blaine reached and entwined their fingers on the table. "Talk to me."

Thank fuck the waiter appeared with the bill and ruined the moment, or Liam would have been unable to stop himself from saying something incredibly stupid.

They paid, the waiter crooned over Blaine, and neither of them was surprised when he blatantly gave Blaine his phone number along with the receipt.

"Let's just go," Liam said, pushing his chair back. "I need a drink and a hot guy all over me."

Was it his imagination, or did Blaine wince at Liam's comment?

In any case, it didn't matter. A trendy bar with strong cocktails, thumping music and a sea of hot, sweaty bodies was exactly what Liam needed.

Chapter seven

The music flowed through every cell in Blaine's body, the bass line mimicking his heartbeat. Time seemed to have slowed since they'd entered the club, the flashing lights in all colours of the rainbow distorting the reality in Blaine's mind. The sexy, shirtless guy currently grinding against him wound his arms around his neck, his crotch pressing against Blaine's. The tight jeans the guy wore left little to the imagination, so Blaine wasn't surprised when, even though the layers of fabric, he could feel his hard cock pressed against Blaine's uninterested one. It was time to let the guy gently down and get another drink at the bar.

A few minutes later, a fresh, cold cocktail in hand, Blaine scanned the crowd for Liam, who'd been dancing with lots of guys all night, barely stopping for a drink. Last time he'd seen him, Liam had been laughing at something a tall, dark-skinned guy was whispering in his ear, his head thrown back, exposing his neck. The guy had taken the opportunity to lick down Liam's exposed skin, before wrapping him in his arms. The throng of bodies had swallowed them then, to Blaine's annoyance.

Blaine clenched his jaw, resisting the urge to stomp around the club, push dancing bodies out of his way until he located Liam and dragged him out. He wanted Liam to have fun on this holiday, he really, *really* did, but he wanted him to have fun with Blaine. They were attracted to each other, that was obvious enough, and had become good friends.

But what if it didn't work out? What if the lustful looks Liam was giving him were just a figment of his imagination? What if the jealousy he'd read in Liam's behaviour at the restaurant was wishful thinking?

Blaine hadn't even told Liam he was bi yet. He hadn't found the right moment. Every time he felt like mentioning it, in his head it sounded forced, like an open invitation.

Would that have even changed anything? Was Liam holding back because he thought Blaine was straight, or because he simply wasn't interested?

And what if Blaine gathered the courage to make a move and Liam shot him down? They were stuck in the same hotel room for the better part of the next two weeks – Blaine couldn't even imagine how awkward they would feel around each other after that. It would ruin the entire trip and Liam would be devastated.

With a shake of his head, Blaine dispersed all those thoughts and allowed the loud music to envelop his senses again. The thumping rhythm seduced him, luring him to finish his drink and dive back into the sweaty, dancing bodies.

Blaine didn't know how much time had passed since he'd surrendered to the music and let it clear his mind of all the questions he had no answers for. In a blur of movement, Liam appeared in front of him, his t-shirt gone, his skin flushed from the heat, his hair a wet mess of unruly curls. And his eyes... His gorgeous light brown eyes sparkled with exhilaration, not even the strobe lights managing to dull the joy in them.

Blaine's entire world shrank to this moment, to the beautiful man in front of him. He wanted to lift his hand and touch Liam's damp skin, feel the heat underneath his fingertips. Instead, he clenched his fists by his sides and aimed a casual smile at him.

"You wanna get out of here?" Liam said in his ear, their chests touching, Liam's heaving with every breath he took. For the briefest of moments Liam's cheek touched Blaine's, a ghost of a contact that sent sparks of desire straight to Blaine's cock.

Closing his eyes, trying to summon enough control to act nonchalant, Blaine opened them to find Liam studying him, his lower lip caught between his teeth. Later, he could always blame the alcohol for his weird behaviour, but right now Blaine couldn't resist lifting his hand to Liam's cheek and stroking it with the tips of his fingers. Liam lowered his lashes, his head leaning into the touch and his body moving closer to Blaine's as if pulled by an invisible magnet.

"Let's go," Blaine whispered in Liam's ear, his hand moving from his cheek to tangle in his hair.

He felt Liam's hand on his hip, his fingers curling into the belt loop of his jeans, pulling him closer. When Liam lifted his lashes, the need in them – the pure, unguarded, unapologetic need – stole Blaine's breath away.

They were standing so close their noses nearly brushed, and yet Blaine felt as if Liam was worlds away. Despite the alcohol clouding his brain, despite the desire exploding in the pit of his stomach, despite Liam's loud and clear invitation, Blaine couldn't cut the last inch between them and kiss him. Not yet. Not until they'd talked and he was certain beyond any doubt where Liam stood.

"Come on," Blaine mouthed, grabbing Liam's hand and twining their fingers.

They left the club hand in hand, the quiet of the early morning startling after the chaos inside. Blaine's ears were still ringing with the ghost of the thumping music, his body still shaking from the adrenalin. The air was warm, but fresh, a welcome breeze cooling their bodies.

"Where's your t-shirt?" Blaine asked, stopping suddenly, making Liam bump into his shoulder.

"I dunno," Liam said with a lazy smile.

Images of Liam dancing with a string of guys flashed in Blaine's mind and he glowered at him.

"When was the last time you had it?" Blaine dropped Liam's hand and folded his arms.

"It's just a t-shirt, Blaine. Don't worry about it."

Blaine wasn't worried about the fucking t-shirt.

"Come on," Liam said, grabbing Blaine's forearm and forcing him to unfold his arms. His hand slid down to Blaine's fingers, tangling with them. "The sun's about to rise. Let's go watch it on the beach."

They walked the short distance to Copacabana beach and sat on the damp sand, watching the night sky as it lightened, various shades of pink, orange, and yellow playing on the horizon. Blaine hugged his knees, the adrenalin draining from his body, fatigue pressing down on him. Liam rested his head on Blaine's shoulder, a content sigh escaping his lips.

"Beautiful," he said, the dreamy quality of the softly spoken word slicing through Blaine's defences.

He didn't even care if Liam had hooked up with someone at the back of the club anymore. After all, he was the one Liam was leaning on right now, and he was the one Liam was going home with, sleeping in his bed, even if they were just friends.

For now.

"For a straight guy you danced with a lot of men tonight," Liam said, breaking the silence and the perfection of the moment.

Blaine's heart skipped a beat, for an entirely different reason.

"Who says I'm straight?" Blaine said, trying to sound casual, but he was holding his breath for Liam's reaction, heart thumping in his chest.

"You were married. To a woman," Liam said, raising his head from Blaine's shoulder.

Blaine turned his head to face him. "I haven't forgotten."

"So, what? You're bi?" A crease of worry appeared between Liam's brows, mistrust darkening his caramel brown eyes.

"I am." Blaine shrugged, looking away.

"And you didn't think to mention that this whole time?"

Blaine didn't like the accusation in Liam's voice.

"It never came up," he stated in a flat, dismissive voice.

Liam snorted, jumping to his feet. "Really, Blaine? It never came up? That's all you have to say?"

Blaine stood up too, not liking the way Liam loomed over him, the beauty of the rising sun entirely forgotten.

"I don't see how this changes anything, *or* is any of your business for that matter."

Liam laughed without humour, his eyes flashing angrily, his fingers curling into fists instinctively. He kept silent for a few moments as if measuring his words carefully, his angry glare unwavering as his jaw muscles clenched.

"I thought we were friends," he finally said through gritted teeth.

"We are."

"Friends trust each other with that kind of information, Blaine. We were practically inseparable for weeks even before we came here, and you never found the right moment to slip in, 'Oh by the way, *babe*, I like fucking men as well as women, FYI.'"

Liam's interpretation of Blaine's voice was so bad he had to bite his lip against a smile. The sight of Liam, shirtless and flustered, his messy curls falling into his eyes and the way they blazed with anger, did Blaine in. He'd never wanted anyone more than he wanted Liam right now.

"Why is this so important to you?" Blaine asked in a soft voice, the fight already draining out of him.

Liam took a step closer, his eyes still blazing, but the anger was dimmed by something else. Something fierce and sexy and determined that tilted Blaine's world on its axis.

"Because I'd have done this a long time ago."

The last word was swallowed between them when their lips met. Before Blaine could figure out what was going on, his arms were welcoming Liam in, instinctively drawing him closer, pressing their bodies together as if they were one. He kissed Liam back, just as desperately, just as urgently, as if making up for lost time. Liam sucked on Blaine's lower lip, then nipped it, before kissing him full on again, tongue exploring, licking, playing with Blaine's own.

Hands fisting in the front of Blaine's t-shirt, Liam kissed him harder, rougher, a strangled moan tearing from his throat. Blaine didn't waver, didn't hesitate, didn't let Liam's desperation scare him away. He tangled his fingers in Liam's hair, keeping him in place, not letting him have any second thoughts about their kiss.

Underneath the lingering sweet flavour of all the cocktails they'd had all night, Liam's taste was even sweeter. His soft moans urged Blaine on, his hand sliding down Liam's back and underneath the waistband of his jeans. Liam gasped, separating their lips, his hooded eyes glowing with wild desire when they met Blaine's.

Blaine caressed the smooth skin on Liam's ass, teasing it before giving it an experimental squeeze. Liam closed his eyes, his body trembling in Blaine's arms as he buried his face in Blaine's neck.

"I want you," Liam whispered, then placed a gentle kiss on Blaine's neck. His fingers untangled from Blaine's t-shirt and he slid them up to Blaine's chest, weaving them around his neck.

I want you.

Three little words Blaine'd wanted to hear ever since he'd met Liam.

Blaine growled, his brain emptying of all doubt, of all reasons why this could potentially turn into a disaster. The need to be with Liam, to touch his bare skin, to kiss him until his lips were swollen, to see him come undone in Blaine's arms, was so powerful, so overwhelming that Blaine was helpless to stop it. It consumed him, burning through his body, making his hands shake as he brought them to Liam's shoulders.

"Let's get out of here," he whispered, pushing Liam gently back to look into his eyes.

The unguarded need in them reflected his own.

In their room, the door barely clicked closed behind them before Blaine pressed Liam against it, claiming his mouth once again. He was starved for Liam's taste, even if they'd stopped to kiss every few steps on their short walk to the hotel. The people monitoring the hotel elevator cameras were probably lighting a cigarette right now after the show they'd given them.

But he couldn't help it. Liam felt so good in his arms, so *right*, as if it was where he should have been all along. Liam snuck his hands under Blaine's t-shirt, fingers digging into bare skin, pulling him impossibly closer. His own skin felt damp and soft under Liam's exploring hands.

Liam bit Blaine's lower lip, then groaned impatiently. "Bed," he whispered, then tried to wiggle free of Blaine's body still pressing him against the door.

Blaine wasn't done with him yet, not by a long shot. By the time they stumbled into bed Liam would be a quivering mess, unable to remember his own name.

Blaine smirked, pulling slightly away, his palms sliding along Liam's forearms until they wrapped around his wrists. Liam gasped, wet lips parting, eyes closing as he leaned his head back against the door. Blaine latched on his throat, tasting the sea and the sunrise on his skin. With a desperate moan Liam tried to pry his wrists free of Blaine's grasp, but he held tight, pulling them off his waist and slamming them against the door. Trapped, Liam was entirely at Blaine's mercy, and judging by the keen moans and the way his body trembled in anticipation, he didn't mind one bit.

"Did you fuck someone at the back of the club?" Blaine asked, unable to stop himself. The thought of someone touching Liam the way he was touching him now, kissing him, making him moan and shiver with need, made Blaine's vision blur with fury.

"No," Liam panted, arching into Blaine. "Didn't want anyone but you, even if I didn't know I could have you."

Blaine met his eyes, and knew beyond a shadow of a doubt Liam was telling the truth. Smiling wickedly as the burden of his jealousy evaporated, Blaine sucked Liam's plump lower lip into his mouth.

"Mmmm, delicious," Blaine murmured as he placed wet kisses along Liam's jaw, then sucked his earlobe into his mouth.

"Stop torturing me," Liam said, trying to pull free again.

"I haven't even started, babe," Blaine said in a husky whisper.

With a loud groan, Liam turned his head, capturing Blaine's lips again. He kissed him slower, deeper, sucking on Blaine's tongue, his hips moving against Blaine's, his hands trembling in Blaine's grasp.

"Fuck," Blaine said, the word coming out of his mouth in a breathless gasp. Liam was too irresistible, too eager, and Blaine found it impossible to keep in control.

Letting go of Liam's wrists, Blaine fell down to his knees and unzipped Liam's jeans with unsteadying fingers. He dragged them down to his knees only to discover Liam was wearing a yellow jockstrap that barely contained his hard cock, a wet spot already forming where precome leaked from the head.

"Goddamn," Blaine said, licking his lips. He raised his eyes to Liam's who was watching him with hooded gaze, unwavering desire burning into his eyes.

Liam buried a hand in Blaine's hair, gently urging him forward. "Suck me," he commanded in a breathless whisper.

Blaine didn't need to be told twice. He mouthed Liam's cock through the thin, silky material of the jockstrap, teasing him, smirking when Liam groaned impatiently. With a swift move of his hand, he pushed the fabric aside, his cock springing free, hitting his belly and leaving a wet trail of precome on his skin.

Blaine licked the length of Liam's cock, his eyes locked on Liam's. Biting his lip, his fingers tightened in Blaine's hair, urging him forward. When Blaine's tongue reached the wet head and tasted the salty precome, he was done for. His eyes rolled back as he greedily swallowed as much of Liam's cock into his mouth as he could manage. Liam was bigger and thicker than average, and Blaine couldn't wait to feel that big cock inside him.

The mere thought of Liam fucking him sent Blaine into mindless oblivion, his own cock so hard inside his jeans that it was ready to burst with a single touch.

It'd been too long. Too fucking long since Blaine had been with someone he didn't want to sneak out on in the middle of the night. Too fucking long since the thought of being fucked excited him.

Liam moaned, the sound desperate and urgent, his legs trembling as Blaine sucked on him, his tongue rolling around the head, his hand sliding up and down his shaft in the same rhythm as his mouth.

"I'm gonna come, Blaine," Liam warned, his voice so strained it was barely audible.

Blaine looked up and saw Liam closing his eyes and leaning back against the door, his fingers playing with a nipple.

"No, you're not," Blaine said, pulling away from Liam's cock.

Liam's eyes shot open, his lips parted and he groaned, his hand sliding down his stomach to his hard, wet shaft. Grabbing his hips, Blaine spun him around, eliciting a surprised grunt. Not giving him a chance to recover, Blaine parted Liam's ass cheeks and plunged his tongue inside.

"Good God!" Liam cried, way past caring who walked by their door. "Fucking hell! If you stop I'm going to kill you," he growled, pushing his ass back into Blaine's eager mouth.

Blaine smiled, his tongue licking at Liam's ass, and his hand sliding down to his own zipper and finally pulling his cock free. He moaned in relief as he wrapped his fist around his shaft, stroking it slowly, keeping his impending orgasm at bay. Liam tasted so good he could eat him for hours.

But neither of them would last hours. They had minutes, at the most. Liam was cursing up a storm, his hand moving on his cock, and his taste was driving Blaine wild. A few faster strokes and he'd be done.

"Ready to come, babe?" Blaine asked, biting Liam's ass cheek hard, then slapping it.

"I've been ready for hours, you bastard," Liam said, his voice hitching on the last word.

He was right where Blaine wanted him. Tightening his grip on his cock, Blaine stroked himself faster, the hot feeling of his impending orgasm burning down his spine. He licked Liam's hole again, slowly flattening his tongue against Liam's flesh, making him shout God's name and a string of curses in the same breath.

Blaine felt Liam's hole clench just as his balls tightened and he came, splattering come all over the door. Blaine was a second behind, a white hot pleasure shooting through his body as he reached his own orgasm.

"Fuck... fuck..." Liam chanted as he tried to catch his breath, his forehead pressed against the door. Blaine could still feel the slight trembling in his body, the aftershocks of his pleasure still coursing through him.

Blaine stood up, wiped his hand on his t-shirt and wrapped it around Liam's waist, pulling him against his chest.

"Now we can go to bed," Blaine whispered in his ear, kissing the soft skin underneath.

Liam smiled lazily, turning his head to meet Blaine's lips.

Chapter eight

Liam stirred, wanting to turn on his back but unable to do so. Consciousness slowly crept in and he squinted an eye open. Blaine had his arms wrapped tightly around him, a leg thrown casually over his thigh, Liam's head tucked under Blaine's chin. If the stiffness in Liam's whole body was anything to go by, they hadn't moved after stumbling into bed in the early hours of the morning.

Awareness of the world around him gradually awoke Liam's tired body and mind. Opening his other eye, he realised the room was dark. What time was it? Surely they hadn't slept more than a few hours – he was still exhausted, but sleeping any more would totally fuck up their schedule.

Speaking of, Liam realised he hadn't even looked at his notebook since they'd arrived. His carefully planned itinerary forgotten on the bottom of his bag.

It was all Blaine's fault. He'd stormed into Liam's life and turned it upside down without even trying. Somehow, Liam couldn't find it in him to be upset about that. Thoughts of the night before – or should he say this morning – swam to the forefront of his mind, bringing with them the lustful haze that always managed to swallow all and any rational thoughts.

After they'd fucked against the door like a couple of horny teenagers, Blaine'd taken Liam's hand and pulled him to the bathroom where they'd shared a much needed shower. And a languid handjob. And a few thousand kisses that made Liam's knees go weak. Then, they'd dried up with a fluffy towel and collapsed into bed. Well, Liam had collapsed. The last thing he remembered was Blaine mumbling something about a 'Do Not Disturb' sign on the door and pulling the blackout curtain shut. Apparently, he'd also turned on the air conditioning and left it on a low setting because the room was pleasantly cool.

The steady rise and fall of Blaine's chest calmed Liam's thoughts, and the warmth from Blaine's body felt good against his skin. The sheets were pooled around their legs, leaving them naked and exposed on the bed.

Exposed to whom?

The moment the thought crossed his mind Liam imagined cameras hidden in every corner of the room and a whole bunch of strangers watching their every move.

With a slight shake of his head, Liam dispersed the ridiculous thoughts, the corners of his mouth lifting as he placed a gentle kiss on Blaine's collarbone. Blaine's skin smelled amazing to Liam's pheromone fogged brain. He couldn't resist a little lick, dying for a taste. It was exactly as he remembered.

And, exactly as he remembered, one taste wasn’t enough.

Liam slid his hand up Blaine’s hip, enjoying the smoothness under his palm. His lips kept kissing every inch of skin he could reach without moving too much. He wanted to wake Blaine with sensual touches and soft kisses, not jolt him awake head butting his chin.

Blaine stirred, his arms tightening around Liam as if on an instinct. He then kissed the top of his head before rolling onto his back and taking Liam with him. Surprised, Liam let out an embarrassing squeal, propping his hands on the mattress on both sides of Blaine’s head to steady himself.

“Mornin’,” Blaine said with a self-satisfied smirk, his hands roaming Liam’s body, finally resting on his ass and squeezing.

Liam leaned down and kissed him instead of a greeting, Blaine’s exploring hands making his already hard cock leak between their bodies. Blaine’s own cock was more than interested in the proceedings, lying hard and proud right under Liam’s.

Slightly pulling away to look into Blaine’s eyes, Liam found them unfocused, dazed, the smirk entirely gone and replaced by an open expression full of need. Not looking away, Blaine brought his hand to his mouth, then sucked his index finger in, making it nice and wet. Liam shivered in anticipation, knowing exactly where the finger was going. When Blaine brought it to Liam's hole, he circled the sensitive spot, tapping it gently without breaching it. Liam shuddered, his arms giving out as he rested his entire weight on top of Blaine.

"Fuck, Blaine, what are you doing to me?" He whispered in Blaine's neck.

Blaine's groan reverberated through Liam's chest, his finger sliding inside him.

Liam whimpered, biting his lip, his hips thrusting against Blaine's on their own accord.

"Grab you cock and jerk yourself off, babe," Blaine said, his voice straining with the effort to speak.

He held Liam tightly against him, one arm wrapped around his waist, the other busy driving him wild. Propping himself up on one hand, Liam snuck the other between them and wrapped his long fingers around both their cocks. Their combined girth was impressive if he said so himself, and he couldn't close his fist, but his grip was tight enough to make Blaine's eyes roll back. He arched off the bed, his Adam's apple working as he tried to swallow. Liam leaned down and licked it, then nipped along Blaine's jaw, all the while working his fist up and down their shafts.

"Fuck, that's good," Blaine managed to say in a husky, low voice that sent a shiver through Liam's body.

"I'm close," Liam whispered, burying his face in the crook of Blaine's neck.

His hips jerked and bucked, Blaine's finger inside him making him lose control. His fist on their cocks sped up, and just when he was about to reach his peak, Blaine curled his finger, finding his magic spot.

The world stopped. Liam's body was nothing but pleasure. For an endless moment nothing existed but the mind-blowing bliss of Blaine's touch.

Awareness slammed into him when Blaine came with a shout, warm liquid spilling over Liam's hand. He opened his eyes to see a reflection of his own pleasure in Blaine's face. His lips were parted and red, swollen from their kisses, his eyes opening to reveal a sinful, lustful blue gaze that tied a tight knot of need inside Liam's belly.

Blaine lifted his head off the pillow and claimed Liam's lips with unguarded urgency, as if they were just starting, not coming down from their orgasms. Without thinking, Liam brought his hand up and tangled his fingers in Blaine's hair, tugging at the strands, trying to bring the man closer. Blaine smiled into the kiss, making Liam pull back to look at him.

"What's funny?" Liam asked breathlessly.

Blaine's eyes danced with amusement, his hands leisurely stroking Liam's back.

"Did you just put jizz in my hair?"

Liam's eyes widened when he realised he had, in fact, smeared jizz all over Blaine's hair.

"I think we're going to need a shower," he said.

"I think you're right." Blaine's expression was wicked, and he emphasised his intentions with a slap on Liam's ass.

"Are we ever going to leave this room?" Liam asked with a raised eyebrow.

"Yes. But not today."

Any sort of protests Liam might have had were swallowed by Blaine's hot, greedy mouth claiming his in a consuming kiss.

In about an hour, they were sitting on the balcony, enjoying the cooling breeze coming from the ocean. The sun wasn't so hot anymore when it was low in the sky, getting ready to hide behind the horizon. Too exhausted to go out for dinner, Blaine had suggested they order room service. What they hadn't planned on, however, was ordering too much food for the tiny table on their balcony. They had to put some of the sides and desserts on the spare chair while they ate in order to accommodate all the dishes.

"This is amazing," Blaine said through a mouth full of steak.

"Ew, gross. Don't talk before you've swallowed your food, pig."

Blaine ignored Liam's comment and gave him a dazzling grin, bits of steak peaking out. Liam rolled his eyes and focused on his own steak. He had to agree – it was really good. Grilled to perfection, coated in some kind of sticky but not overly sweet marinade, the tender meat melting on his tongue. He'd have been perfectly happy with only ordering the steaks, but apparently Blaine turned into a beast that thought he could eat a mammoth when hungry, and ordered half the menu. They had French fries, three different kinds of salad, steamed rice and freshly baked garlic bread.

To call Blaine's food choice eclectic would be an understatement, but he wouldn't listen to reason when Liam suggested all this food might be a bit too much. He'd glared at him, still clutching the hotel phone in his hand, and ordered four different kinds of dessert.

Liam sipped from his water, his gaze darting towards the ocean. It was late and yet there were a lot of people still lounging around, playing sports, laughing with their friends, kids running around chasing after balls, or flying kites. His thoughts drifted inward to all the doubt and reservations he'd had about being with Blaine.

Sex with Blaine was mind-blowing, there was no denying that. It'd also felt good to wake up in Blaine's arms. There was no panic, no anxiety, no need to find an explanation why it'd felt so right.

But now... Now they needed to talk.

"Hey," Blaine said softly, entwining his fingers with Liam's on the table. "Everything okay?"

Liam nodded. Everything *was* okay, but he needed to straighten some things out with Blaine.

"Do you want to stash the desserts in the fridge and go for a walk on the beach?" Liam asked, squeezing Blaine's hand when he frowned.

"Sure."

They quickly packed away all the desserts and leftovers for a late night snack, threw the rubbish in the bin, and made their way to Ipanema across the road. The sand was still warm beneath their feet as they removed their flip-flops and walked barefoot towards the water. People were packing their stuff and leaving now that the sun was half way behind the horizon, and Liam was glad they'd have a bit more privacy.

Holding his flip-flops in one hand, Blaine reached for Liam's hand with the other, in a gesture so casual it made Liam's stomach flutter. They tangled their fingers and kept walking in silence, Blaine patiently waiting for Liam to form his thoughts.

"I..." Liam started, then paused, clearing his throat, still unsure of what exactly to say. Blaine tightened his fingers in his. "I love being with you, and I'd be lying if I said that I wasn't imagining what we did last night – and more – so many times since the day I met you." Liam paused again, daring a sideways glance at Blaine. There was no visible reaction to his words, apart from a muscle jumping in Blaine's jaw as he kept staring straight ahead. "But I'm not looking for anything beyond casual sex right now."

Liam closed his eyes, the words sounding harsh even to his own ears.

It wasn't strictly true. Blaine wasn't just a random hook up. He liked the guy, they'd become good friends in such a short time, and for reasons unknown, Liam felt like he belonged when he was with Blaine. The sex last night didn't feel awkward at all; it felt like the natural progression of their relationship.

But Liam couldn't say that. Blaine was a victim of circumstance – he was here, in one of the most romantic, gorgeous, sexy cities in the entire world because of Liam. Would they have hooked up if they were still in London? If Blaine wasn't tied to Liam, forced to share a hotel room with him?

"Why is that?" Blaine's voice sounded casual, as if he wasn't bothered at all by what Liam'd said.

Liam furrowed his brows and looked away from Blaine. "I've never been in a relationship that didn't end with me getting hurt, and I'm tired of it," he said, knowing Blaine deserved the truth, not some half-assed excuse.

Liam waited for Blaine to say something but he kept silent, staring straight ahead, still holding his hand as if he deserved it.

"My first time was with my best friend. We were still kids, I was fifteen and he was sixteen," Liam said with a sigh. He might as well spill all the beans and be done with it. "We were dating in secret for two years because he was afraid to come out to his parents. And then he decided he wasn't really gay, and dumped me before he went to college. I got angry and said some things to him I'm not really proud of, and he got scared I'd out him and punched me. But what hurt worse than his fist was that he threw our friendship away without a moment's hesitation. Then he told me I was just an available hole for him to stick his dick in and nothing more. Those were his last words to me. He never tried to get in touch later and apologise. I guess he wasn't really sorry for what he'd said because it was true – I found out he got married three years ago."

Blaine stopped walking and turned to face Liam. In the dim light of the twilight he was even more beautiful than usual – the blue in his eyes was darker, much like the depths of the ocean behind him; the stubbled jaw reminding Liam of his rough kisses.

"I'm sorry," Blaine said, then bit his lip as if preventing himself from saying anything else.

Liam sighed. "It's fine. I was just a kid, didn't know any better." He swallowed hard, remembering all the times after that when he hadn't known any better, only to end up being humiliated and hurt simply because he'd trusted someone with his heart. "That's not all, though. I've been fucked in the closet, cheated on, dumped for a woman – you name it. And yet, I keep looking for love, getting hurt over and over."

He let go of Blaine's hand and raked it through his hair. He hadn't meant to say so much when they left the hotel, but in a way he was glad Blaine knew. He felt the prickling behind his eyes, and hated his traitorous body for displaying his emotions so clearly. He tried to look away but Blaine stopped him with a hand on his cheek.

"Hey," he said gently, stroking a thumb over his cheekbone. "I'm not asking for your hand in marriage, okay?" He smiled, and Liam couldn't help but give him a watery grin in return. "I signed my divorce papers a few weeks before we came here, remember? Even if my marriage was over long before that, I'm not ready for any sort of a relationship yet."

Liam nodded, both relieved and a little disappointed. His stupid fucking heart was hoping Blaine would somehow convince him to try. How many times did it need to be broken before it learned its lesson?

"But we're here on a romantic trip together, and we like each other, we have a great time together. And," Blaine grinned wolfishly, leaning in closer to Liam. "We have great chemistry in bed." He brushed his lips over Liam's in a ghost of a kiss that knocked the oxygen out of Liam's lungs.

Behind him, the waves kept crashing on the shore as if nothing was happening. As if Liam's world wasn't turning upside down.

"Yeah, we do," Liam said, trying to sound casual, even managing a little smirk.

"So how about we stop overanalysing everything and take it one day at a time? Holiday bubble, remember?" Blaine winked at him and kissed the tip of his nose.

"What about when we get back to London?" Liam asked.

"We'll figure it out when we get there, okay?" Blaine moved his hand from Liam's cheek to the back of his neck, pulling him closer, their lips nearly touching as he spoke. "We can keep it casual or be just friends. We can do whatever you want."

"What do *you* want?" Liam asked in a breathless whisper, barely controlling the urge to sneak his tongue out and lick Blaine's lips.

"I'm fine with casual," Blaine said with a little shrug, but a shadow passed behind his eyes. He blinked and it was gone, a smile tugging on his lips instead. "I don't think I'll ever want to kick you out of my bed, baby." The smile grew, his eyes twinkling. "But if you get sick of me and want to be just friends, I'll learn to live with it."

Liam smiled, the weight on his chest lifting a little. He felt like he could tell Blaine anything; he'd felt that way ever since that first day he'd met him. There was something about him that made Liam feel safe. It was weird and totally unreasonable, but there you go. You couldn't control the weird shit you felt, could you?

"Speaking of..." Liam said, giving in to the urge to kiss Blaine. It was a short, soft kiss, just to whet the appetite for later. "Do you want to go back to the hotel? We need to get a good night's rest because tomorrow we'll be sightseeing, and I have a ton of stuff planned."

Blaine groaned dramatically before kissing Liam. "Fine," he said with an exasperated sigh.

Liam grinned, wrapped an arm around Blaine's waist and headed back to the hotel.

Chapter nine

I'm fine with casual? What the fuck was he thinking saying that? He was a hundred percent not fucking fine with casual!

Blaine turned on his side, careful not to jostle Liam too much, and snuck out of bed. He tiptoed to the bathroom and closed the door behind him before switching the light on. Turning the cold water tap on, Blaine splashed his face, hoping to get rid of all the jumbled thoughts in his head.

"What are you doing?" He whispered to his reflections, knowing he wouldn't magically find any answers, but searching the blue eyes staring back at him nonetheless.

He needed a plan. He'd lied to Liam for a reason. The deer in the headlights look Liam'd given him after he'd confessed about his disastrous relationships had been heartbreaking. If Blaine'd babbled about how much he liked him and how he wanted so much more than sex from him, and how much he hoped what was happening here between them was only the beginning, Liam would have bolted. And just like that his dream holiday would be ruined.

So, yeah, he'd lied. He didn't need time. He knew what he wanted, and that was Liam, and if pretending that this was nothing more than two guys having fun, then so be it. But once they were back in London, all bets were off.

In the meantime, he'd woo Liam and show him what they could have together. After all, they were in Rio. He'd show him that being in love wasn't something to fear, even if it did feel a little scary to trust someone with your heart.

But Blaine would always protect Liam's heart, even at the expense of his own.

Mind made up, Blaine felt a little calmer. He splashed his face again, then dried it with a towel before walking quietly out of the bathroom. Sneaking back into bed, he spooned Liam from behind and wrapped his arms around his warm body, before letting Liam's soft breathing lull him to sleep.

When he'd said he had a ton of stuff planned, Liam hadn't been joking. It wasn't even noon yet and they'd already visited several museums and art galleries in the city centre, and were heading to Corcovado to see Christ the Redeemer statue, and then to the top of Sugar Loaf mountain. Liam's aunt had told him it was best to go to Sugar Loaf in the evening on a clear day and watch the sun set over Rio.

As good as all that sounded, Blaine wanted to do back to the beach and do absolutely nothing all day.

But Liam had been full of smiles today, taking photos of every little thing – and hundreds of Blaine – and so full of joy and energy that it was starting to rub off on Blaine. Maybe seeing the sun set over Rio wouldn't be so bad.

"You okay?" Liam asked, gently touching his upper arm.

They were on the back seat of a taxi, the driver weaving through traffic like a maniac while talking on the phone and checking his incoming bookings on a screen on the dash. Blaine actually felt a little sick.

"Yeah. Just scared for my life." He grabbed Liam's hand when the taxi lurched forward, drag racing all other cars at the traffic light.

"It's all part of the experience," Liam said, and when Blaine turned to face him with a look of annoyance on his face, Liam had his camera up and snapped a photo. "That's going on Instagram as soon as I get WiFi," he said with a smirk.

Blaine rolled his eyes just as the taxi pulled to a stop, slamming on the breaks. Apparently, they'd arrived at their destination.

Blaine couldn't get out of the car fast enough, while Liam paid and asked the driver in broken Portuguese which way the tram to the summit was. The guy pointed across the road from where they were standing and sped off.

Undeterred, Liam snapped a photo of the taxi, then grabbed Blaine's hand and crossed the road. The little funicular railway station was quickly filling up with people. It would take them to the top of the mountain to see the most famous statue of the world. Thankfully, Liam had researched what to do and headed straight for the ticket office where he managed to buy the last two tickets for the next tram. The American behind him wasn't too pleased to have been told he needed to wait for the next service.

The red tram was full to the brim when it started its journey up to the top of the mountain. Liam sat next to the window, courteously offering Blaine the place first. Considering all the windows in the tram were down and they were about to go up on a very steep hill, the path barely big enough for the tram, Blaine declined.

Blaine didn't deal well with heights. And all of Rio's sights seemed to be really fucking high.

Liam snapped pictures, smiling behind the camera the whole time. As the tram progressed up the hill, the view opening to its passengers was spectacular. Blaine tried to ignore the straight drop to certain death right next to the tram, and focused on the bird's eye view of Rio.

When that didn't help with his sweating palms and impending panic attack, he focused on Liam. As if sensing his discomfort, Liam turned to him and snapped a photo, then positioned them close together, turning the camera on both of them for a selfie. Blaine smiled, his worries nearly forgotten.

Liam put the lens cap back in place and let the camera rest on the strap around his neck. He held Blaine's hand, and started chatting about the history of the tiny railway, rattling off statistics for how many services there were per day, how many people it could carry, why there were stops along the way even though they were in a forest and there was practically nothing around, and God knew what else. Blaine stopped listening to the words at some point, letting Liam's voice calm his speeding pulse.

Before he knew it, the tram arrived at the top of Corcovado and everyone rushed towards the doors.

"Thank you," Blaine said, squeezing Liam's hand.

Liam simply smiled in return, holding Blaine's eyes for a few long moments, before jerking his chin towards the doors.

"Let's go."

Christ the Redeemer was everything Blaine thought it would be – big and majestic, a lone figure watching over the entire city. But it was also simple, and elegant, the clean lines of the statue not taking anything away from its splendour, but rather making it even more imposing. The views from the top were incredible, and Blaine felt better looking over Rio when there was a thick, concrete wall separating him from a steep drop.

"It's amazing, isn't it?" Blaine heard Liam's voice right next to him, the shutter of the camera clicking when Blaine turned his head.

"Yeah," Blaine said with a smile, his eyes darting towards the views of Rio beneath him.

The lakes, the beaches, the huge parks, hills and valleys – it all came together in a breathtaking picture, forever imprinted on Blaine's mind. He thought he was starting to understand what the big deal about Rio was. If he couldn't tear his eyes away from it now, how was he ever supposed to leave?

"You're falling in love right now, aren't you?" Liam said, his camera clicking relentlessly.

Blaine turned to face him, his eyes sliding past Liam to the view of Copacabana beach behind him, and then back on Liam's face.

"Yeah," he finally said, feeling his cheeks flushing. "I think I am."

The tram to the top of Corcovado had nothing on the cable car to the top of Sugar Loaf mountain. It was terrifying. The slope was so steep it actually made Blaine's eyes cross when he looked down a few minutes after they departed.

"That hike you mentioned earlier sounds better and better right now," he said, placing his head on Liam's shoulder as they sat inside the cable car.

"Really? You want to *walk* that?" Liam pointed at the very, *very* steep hill they were currently flying over.

"Fuck," Blaine whispered, raking a trembling hand through his hair. "I don't want to be here at all, actually. What's wrong with the beach?"

Liam looked at him, concern in his gorgeous eyes, and Blaine felt like a total wanker.

"I'm sorry," he hastened to say, not giving Liam any opportunity to regret their sightseeing trip. "I didn't mean that." He straightened, placing a hand on Liam's thigh. "I just don't deal well with heights."

"I've noticed," Liam raised an eyebrow. "You do look quite pale." He brought his backpack on his lap and took out a bottle of water and a banana, handing them to Blaine. "Here. That should do for now, and we can have late lunch when we get to the top."

Blaine took the bottle gratefully, chugging down half of it in one go. He tried to focus on the people around them instead of the ground beneath them, which was a very fucking long way down.

Right. People around them.

The cable car was quite large and there were a few more people in it, but not too many to make it crowded. It seemed like there were two groups – a family with three kids, and a group of friends. The family didn't say much, but Blaine thought he recognised a few Spanish words when the mum spoke to her eldest. The friends group spoke rapidly in a language Blaine couldn't place.

None of them seemed to mind that they were practically caught in a death trap, a million miles above ground, resisting gravity by sheer luck, and not all that stable looking steel rope.

"We're nearly there," Liam whispered in his ear, putting the untouched banana back in his bag.

Thank fucking God.

The air was pleasantly cool on top of the mountain when they finally exited the cable car. Blaine felt immediately better once they left the fucking thing behind. The views from here were a bit different than on top of Corcovado. For starters, they seemed to be a bit lower this time, and right next to the ocean.

"That's Guanabara Bay," Liam said, placing his elbows on the steel railing next to Blaine.

It was beautiful. Peaceful. A few white yachts were anchored in the bay, their sails rippling in the breeze, and more floated leisurely in the ocean beyond. The sun was low in the sky, getting ready to hide behind the horizon soon, but its rays still played with the water, making it sparkle.

"Come on, let's walk a full circle," Liam said, reaching for Blaine's hand and enveloping it in his.

The warm, dry skin of Liam's palm anchored Blaine to the moment, not letting his thoughts drift too far away. They walked around the cobblestone path, Liam taking pictures with his camera, and Blaine with his phone. A helicopter zoomed passed them, a movement so sudden and loud Blaine wasn't sure where it came from. Startled, he followed its flight until it landed on a helicopter pad right beneath the railing. A man and a woman got out of the helicopter, their clothes flapping in the wind the spinning blades created.

Blaine looked on, still horrified people actually paid money to be trapped in that tiny machine that looked like it could be blown away by a gust of wind. When he heard Liam's camera clicking behind him, Blaine turned to find Liam lowering the camera and looking at the helicopter with what can only be described as longing.

"No. Fucking. Way." Blaine pronounced every word loudly and clearly, making another tourist turn around and scowl at him, then proceed to tug his wife away from the hooligans.

"But..." Liam started, his eyes drifting back to the helicopter that was now taking off.

"No."

Blaine grabbed Liam's hand and pulled him away before he got any other dumb ideas.

Soon, they'd walked around the whole place, ending up pretty much where they'd started, and Blaine hadn't seen any restaurant or cafes.

"Where are we supposed to have that lunch you mentioned?"

"On top of Sugar Loaf," Liam said distractedly, staring at the camera's display and frowning.

Blaine looked around, confused. "You mean, here?"

Liam took his eyes off the screen and looked at Blaine as if he'd lost his mind.

"This is not Sugar Loaf, honey," he said, smirking when Blaine narrowed his eyes. Liam never used endearments, he was up to something. "*This* is Sugar Loaf." He pointed towards a huge fucking mountain right behind Blaine's back.

Blaine turned and took an instinctive step back. The mountain behind him was high and narrow, and connected to the hill they currently stood at with a few ropes. Steel ropes. A cable car leisurely travelled on one of the ropes, gently swaying in the wind. It looked like a white dot in the sky.

"I showed you where we were going from the top of Corcovado. This is just the summit on the way to the top of Sugar Loaf. We still have a way to go." Liam looped his arm around Blaine's and tugged him towards the cable car station behind the corner.

Blaine was too stunned to speak. He'd seen the mountain from Corcovado, true, but it didn't look that damn high. Or maybe Blaine's fear of heights was making everything seem bigger than it actually was. He didn't fucking know. All he knew was that he wasn't sure he'd survive another cable car ride over a hundred mile drop.

"You'll be fine," Liam said, kissing his cheek.

Blaine really doubted that.

The cable car was smaller than the previous one, there were no seats, and everyone was crowded in the tiny space, craning their necks to look out the floor to ceiling windows. It moved faster than Blaine anticipated, the sway from the air current that high above making him even more nervous. He held on to the pole in the middle of the car, his eyes shut firmly. If he didn't look, it wasn't so bad.

"Have you ever seen a rainforest in real life?" Liam whispered in his ear, his hand gently moving up and down his upper arm.

Blaine squinted one eye open and followed Liam's finger pointing at the green trees beneath them. The forest was thick and lush, different shades of green blending in the sunshine.

Liam started telling Blaine about the kinds of animals, birds, and butterflies that could be seen in the forest if you decided to do the hike instead of the cable car. He kept talking about the rainforest and how it used to cover the whole of Rio de Janeiro, but now only survived on the mountain. And how if you came here right after it'd rained, the air was so clear and it smelled so fresh, like nothing you'd ever experienced.

Blaine wasn't looking at the rainforest or the mountain or the bird's eye view of Rio beneath him anymore. He was looking at Liam, his warm brown eyes that twinkled with joy; absorbing his low, husky voice, feeling it spread over his insides like honey.

The thought that crossed his mind was unexpected, but not unwelcome.

I'll take you for a hike in the rain someday.

He really planned on keeping that promise.

The cable car jerked to a stop, breaking the moment. Liam stopped talking and smiled at Blaine, obviously pleased with himself that he'd managed to distract Blaine from his fears.

"Come on, you've earned your food. Let's go feed you." He winked and entwined his fingers with Blaine's again as if it was the most natural thing in the world.

They ate at the cosy cafe, the views of Rio spread beneath them, the sounds of birds, insects, and animals coming from the forest relaxing Blaine until his terrifying experience coming here was all but a distant memory. After they finished their sandwiches, they ordered a couple of iced lattes, but took them to go. Walking around, Blaine sipped from his cold drink and gazed around, trying to remember every detail from the spectacular scenery all around him.

"Look!" Liam exclaimed in a hushed voice. "A monkey! It's probably a marmoset, they're pretty common here in the rainforest."

Blaine remembered Liam talking about wild marmosets and all kinds of birds and insects on the way up here. They stepped closer, trying to not scare it off. It didn't seem to be afraid, watching them with its beady eyes, elegantly perched on a branch right above the railing.

Liam took out the banana he still carried in his backpack, peeled it and offered the little monkey a piece. It took it greedily with its little fingers and immediately tucked into it, still watching them cautiously.

Liam turned to Blaine and beamed, slowly taking out his camera and snapping a hundred photos of the monkey. It seemed to be pretty used to impromptu photo sessions from awed tourists, because it didn't seemed concerned in the slightest. If anything it adjusted its sitting angle so that the camera caught its good side.

"Go closer to it and I'll snap a picture," Blaine suggested.

Liam stepped closer, moving slowly not to scare it away, and Blaine took out his phone to take several photos. By the time he was done, the monkey had eaten its banana and was looking at Liam expectantly.

Liam rolled his eyes and gave it the rest of the fruit, while Blaine captured the moment the monkey stretched its arms to get it from Liam's hand. Satisfied there was no more to be gained from this particular pair of tourists, the monkey hopped off the branch and disappeared out of view.

"That was pretty cool," Blaine said, putting the phone back in his pocket.

"Come. We have to get going or we'll miss it." Liam grabbed Blaine's hand again and strode purposefully round the corner.

Blaine didn't even bother asking where they were going. It seemed like Liam had everything prepared and he was just along for the ride. He didn't mind one bit.

Liam led him down a flight of stairs to a little alcove tucked away from the main path. It was right next to the railing, but off the beaten path so it was pretty secluded. Removing his bag, he dropped it on the ground and leaned back against the wall. Blaine came to do the same, managing to squeeze next to him in the tiny space.

Liam slurped from his latte, pointing at the view stretched in front of them. Beaches, hills, forests, and lakes lay beneath them, houses and blocks of flats scattered between them. In the distance, the sun was low on the horizon, its orange halo too bright to look at for longer than a few seconds.

"I promised you a sunset over Rio de Janeiro," Liam said, leaving his now empty cup on the ground. "Here it is."

Ever so slowly, the sun descended behind the horizon, its bright light reflecting over any surface. The water gleamed with orange specks jumping from one wave to another; the windows in the high buildings shimmering as if about to burst into tiny pieces of light; the trees in the forest reflecting the light in all shades green.

It was a stunning, magical view that Blaine could never get tired of.

Just as he turned to share that with Liam, he found him watching Blaine instead of the sunset. He was close, so close that if Blaine parted his lips their breaths would mingle. His eyes were a paler shade of honey, absorbing the orange glow from the sun and claiming it as their own.

"Liam..." Blaine said, the name more like an exhale than an actual word.

He didn't know how to continue. All he knew was that this moment right now was the happiest he'd ever been.

Pressing his lips to Blaine's, Liam didn't give him a chance to speak. The kiss was slow and wet, exploratory and giving at the same time. Blaine cupped the back of Liam's neck and pulled him closer, feeling Liam's fingers digging into his hips. Liam whimpered when Blaine nipped his lower lip, then sucked on it before delving deep into the kiss again.

How was he supposed to keep this casual when his soul was already mated to Liam's?

Didn't Liam feel this way too?

A loud static noise made them jump apart as if shot by a taser. Liam grimaced, wiping his mouth with the back of his hand as a voice followed the noise and announced on several languages that the last cable car back down was in ten minutes and everyone should be on it.

Blaine looked around to see the sun had almost set, only a sliver of orange light still visible behind the horizon. How long had they been kissing? It felt like he'd fallen asleep only to wake up to a brand new reality.

"We should go," Liam said, bending down to pick up his bag and empty cup.

"Yeah." Blaine picked up his own cup, still a bit dazed. "Liam?" He said, and Liam faced him. "Thanks. For all this today." He spread his arms wide as if thanking Liam for Rio de Janeiro itself. In a way, Liam had given him Rio in all its glory, hadn't he? "I know I acted like a twat and moaned all the time, but I really enjoyed this. I'm glad I got to see all of Rio with you."

Liam beamed at him, taking a step closer and kissing his cheek. His mouth lingered, and then he rubbed the tip of his nose on Blaine's cheekbone. The move was so graceful, so feline-like, that Blaine itched to pull him in his arms again. But there was no time.

"You're welcome," Liam murmured before pulling Blaine behind him to get on the last cable car service for the day.

Blaine grinned like an idiot, walking behind Liam and not even minding that he'd have to experience the whole terrifying ride again.

Much.

Chapter ten

When they got back to the hotel, Blaine flopped face down on the bed and refused to move. Liam was tired, too, but also hungry, so he settled on room service. Liam ordered the food and a bottle of wine, and headed for the bathroom to take a shower, leaving Blaine to his power nap.

The hot water felt good on his aching body. He'd had an amazing day, soaking in the magic of Rio de Janeiro like a dried out sponge. But it was good to finally be taking a little rest, putting aside all the impressions and feelings in his jumbled brain.

For the moment, he was too exhausted to try and analyse why Blaine was kissing him as if he never wanted to stop, and why he was already starting to miss Rio even though he was still here.

His shower must have taken longer than anticipated because by the time he walked out of the bathroom in a cloud of steam, Blaine was arranging the food on the table outside. Without bothering to get dressed, Liam walked out on the balcony only in the towel wrapped around his waist, revelling in the cooler night air hitting his damp skin.

"You're not going to get dressed?" Blaine asked when Liam plonked in the heavily cushioned chair.

"Nope." He picked a French fry from the plate in front of him, savouring the salty taste as it hit his taste buds. Of course, he couldn't stop at one, so he took a couple more and stuffed them into his mouth all at once.

Blaine made a weird sound, forcing Liam to drag his gaze from the food to his face. A muscle in Blaine's jaw ticked and his lips thinned as he glared at Liam.

"What?" Liam asked, looking down at his chest to check if he had food on it or something.

Blaine sighed and looked up at the sky. "At least wait until all the food is laid out."

Liam didn't. He stuffed more fries in his mouth, and tried to grab a piece of the pizza, but that got his hand swatted away.

"I'm hungry," he whined, then pouted for good measure.

"I can tell. You ordered the entire menu."

"You were sleeping, so I didn't know what you'd like."

"I wasn't sleeping, I just couldn't be bothered to gather enough energy to argue with you over garlic bread."

Liam mumbled a 'whatever' before picking an extra long fry from his plate, eating it intentionally slowly, watching Blaine as he set the rest of the food out and took a seat in the chair across from him. Liam would be lying if he said he didn't enjoy the way

Blaine's eyes slid over his body, the way that sexy jaw muscle jumped when Liam caught him staring.

"Can I eat now, your majesty?" Liam asked, too hungry to care about the art of seduction right now.

Blaine ignored him, not that he actually waited for an answer before he piled food on his plate and dug in.

Blaine mumbled something that suspiciously sounded like, 'And then he says I'm a pig', but, following his example, Liam ignored him.

Liam hadn't realised how hungry he was until he started eating. That sandwich had been a mere distraction from the hunger, and they'd barely eaten anything else all day. Blaine was focused on his food, too, and they ate in comfortable silence, occasionally taking a sip from the chilled wine.

Blaine's knee brushed Liam's under the table and he really tried to ignore it, but he was starting to feel intensely aware that he wasn't dressed. As if reading his mind, Blaine shifted, leaning back in his chair and stretching his legs on the outside of the table. His head fell back on the chair, and he closed his eyes with a content sigh.

Liam had the sudden urge to remove the towel and straddle Blaine's thighs.

"So," he cleared his throat, trying to distract himself with conversation.

Blaine opened his eyes lazily half way, and looked at Liam, patiently waiting for him to continue.

Liam usually forgot his own name when that blue gaze was focused so intensely on him, and this time was no exception.

"You have to send me some of those photos you took today," Blaine said after a long pause that made Liam blush.

"Sure. But tomorrow?" Liam followed Blaine's example and leaned back into his chair. The hammock on the other side of the balcony was starting to look more and more appealing. "I'm exhausted right now, I can't even be bothered to check my email."

"So you haven't seen Instagram yet?"

Liam shook his head.

"I posted some pictures from today's sightseeing and the last couple of days on the beach, and one from the club," Blaine said, his lazy smile growing into a full blown grin. "Apparently, people like you. A lot."

"My curiosity is officially piqued," Liam said, standing up.

His towel had loosened while he'd been sitting and it slipped precariously low on his hips.

"Oops," Liam said, catching the towel right before it slipped down completely.

A low growl came from Blaine's general direction and before he could blink, Liam was pressed against the balcony railing, caged in Blaine's arms.

"You've been teasing me with the fucking towel all evening," Blaine said in a low, sexy voice that sent a shiver down Liam's body.

He could deny it. He could say he'd been too tired to get dressed, or that he hadn't realised he was teasing him. But they'd both know he was lying. Liam'd enjoyed Blaine's eyes on him way too much to even try to be subtle about it.

"Are you complaining?" Liam asked, arching an eyebrow.

Blaine leaned closer, their chests touching. He removed his hand from the railing and deliberately, slowly, untucked the towel from its loose knot. Before it could fall to the floor, Blaine grabbed both ends and spread it on the railing, shielding Liam's naked ass from any curious looks

"Not at all," Blaine whispered, sneaking his tongue out to lick Liam's lower lip.

Liam wrapped his arms around Blaine's neck and pressed their bodies even closer together as they kissed, Liam's naked erection rubbing against Blaine's jeans. He craved to touch Blaine's bare skin, but the fact that Blaine was fully clothed while Liam was naked and at his mercy, was very arousing.

Blaine broke their kiss with a grunt, resting his head on Liam's shoulder.

"I have to go take a quick shower," he said. "You're all nice and fresh, and I smell like a donkey." He spread his fingers on Liam's ribs, the warm touch of his palm imprinting on Liam's skin.

"I like how you smell," Liam said, kissing the side of Blaine's neck and rubbing his nose against his skin.

"As flattering as that is," Blaine began, lifting his head and placing a soft peck on Liam's lips. "The things I want to do to you require a bit more hygiene. After all, you did drag me through all of Rio today."

"Fine," Liam grumbled with an expressive eye roll.

Blaine smiled, kissed him again, then grabbed his hand and pulled him inside. Promising to be super fast in the shower, he undressed quickly and sauntered to the bathroom. Liam lay naked on the bed, stroking his cock absently, thinking how good Blaine must look in the shower, all wet and slick and soapy...

Before he knew it, exhaustion mixed with his fantasies, and he was drifting to sleep, still imagining Blaine under the hot water.

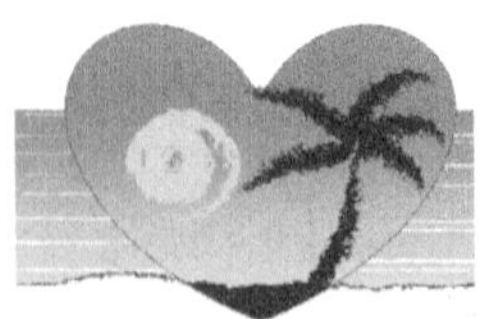

"I fucking knew it," Blaine mumbled under his breath, trying not to wake Liam.

Closing the bathroom door gently behind him, Blaine lay next to Liam on the bed, wrapping an arm around his waist. The guy didn't even stir. He was snoring softly, his body relaxed under Blaine's arm.

With a sigh, Blaine snuggled closer, kissing the freckles on Liam's shoulder. There would be plenty of time for sex in the morning. But for now... For now, this was enough.

Blaine woke up to the blissful feeling of Liam's mouth around his cock. He'd barely opened his eyes when the pleasure slammed into him, blindsiding him, and he came with Liam's name on his lips. What followed was a few preciously intimate moments of tangled limbs, whispered words, lips seeking lips, sweat slicked skin under urgent fingertips.

Liam shuddered in Blaine's arms, his soft mewling moans swallowed by Blaine's eager mouth. The room was dark and quiet, their heavy breathing filling the entire space.

Liam didn't seem like he wanted to move even, if they both needed a shower. He wrapped an arm around Blaine's waist and snuggled closer, chest to chest, lips pressing soft kisses on Blaine's neck. Blaine pulled the thin blanket over them and swung a leg over Liam's thighs, trapping him in the embrace.

"Mornin'," Liam mumbled against Blaine's skin.

"Good morning to you, too," Blaine said with a wide smile. "Were you trying to make up for falling asleep on me last night?"

Liam chuckled. "Nah, you took too long in the shower, it's your own damn fault." Blaine huffed in response, but didn't protest. He buried his fingers in Liam's hair, gently massaging his scalp. "I woke up horny and saw you were hard, and couldn't resist." Liam purred as Blaine's fingers played with his hair, the sound shooting straight to Blaine's cock. "What were you dreaming about?" Liam asked, hand sliding to Blaine's neck, thumb stroking his stubbled jaw.

"Don't remember."

Liam hummed, lifting his head a little to look at Blaine. "This will sound really weird after I just said I woke up really horny, but I dreamt I had a dog."

Blaine chuckled, leaning in to place a soft kiss on Liam's lips.

"What was its name?"

"I don't know, but it was a big dog, kinda shaggy, with the biggest brown eyes I've ever seen. We went for a walk and there was a lake in the distance, and it ran towards the water. I tried to call its name, or run after it, but I couldn't move and no sound came out of my mouth. And then, just on the edge of the water, the dog stopped, turned to look at me like it was trying to tell me something, and then jumped in the lake. I woke up with a sense of anxiety, as if something bad was about to happen and I couldn't do anything to stop it."

Blaine kept stroking Liam's hair, playing with the soft strands, enjoying the low rumble of Liam's voice against his skin.

"Have you ever had a dog?" Blaine asked.

Liam shook his head. "No. Mum always worked long hours and we moved a lot, so she never agreed to get one, even though I begged for years. I was desperate for a dog when I was a kid. I never had many friends and I used to imagine me with a dog, running around and causing all kinds of trouble."

"What about your dad?"

"I've never met him. He got my mum pregnant at seventeen and when she refused to get an abortion he dumped her."

"I'm sorry," Blaine said, kissing his temple.

"It's okay," Liam said when the tender kiss ended. "I had a lovely childhood even if we moved every couple of years or so. But my mum is great, and she worked her ass off to make sure I had everything I needed, and she was always there for me, you know? She still is."

Blaine kissed him again, unable to stop himself. Their lips nearly brushed as Liam talked, how was he supposed to resist these perfect, pouty lips?

But he kept the kiss gentle and short, wanting Liam to keep talking. He rarely talked about his personal life, but in this moment, in the quiet of the dawn, Liam was opening up and saying things he wouldn't share in the bright light of day.

"Are you close to your folks?" Liam asked, placing a kiss on Blaine's jaw and snuggling into him again.

"Yeah, I guess." Liam didn't say anything, but his silence encouraged Blaine to continue. "They're kinda weird," he said with a fond smile.

Blaine felt Liam smile against his neck, before he said, "The apple doesn't fall far from the tree."

Blaine squeezed his ass, hard, and Liam nipped at his jaw in retaliation.

"Weird how?" Liam asked after kissing the bitten flesh.

"They live in a cottage in Norfolk that they designed themselves. Had it built on a plot of land they bought even before I was born. Ever since I was a kid I remember them planning, saving money, day dreaming about building their own house and being as self-sufficient as possible, with their own wind turbine, solar panels, all that stuff. As a teenager I thought it was stupid." Blaine smiled at the thought, remembering how his mother's blue eyes sparkled every time she talked about her beloved cottage. "But now I love going there to decompress. I always gain at least five pounds, though. Mum's cooking does that to you. She has a vegetable garden, a small orchard, and Dad insisted on getting chicken. I think the only food they actually buy is meat and dairy, they produce everything else themselves."

Liam listened, his fingers making lazy circles on Blaine's shoulder, his breathing slowing as Blaine talked. He didn't comment, but his cheeks moved against Blaine's chest and he knew Liam was smiling.

"I can't stand being there for more than a week at a time, though. The fucking serenity drives me up a wall. They do yoga every day at the break of dawn, for fuck's sake."

Liam laughed softly, his breath tickling Blaine's skin. Blaine wanted to keep talking, but he didn't know what else to say. His family was pretty boring, no big drama to keep things interesting. He wanted Liam to share more about his life, but he didn't want to push.

After a few silent moment Liam asked, "Do they know you're bi?"

"Yeah."

"I guess they don't have any problem with it?"

"Not at all. They always said they didn't care who I was with as long as he or she respected me and made me happy. When my marriage fell apart Mum and Dad were my rock."

Liam tensed in Blaine's arms at the mention of his marriage.

"What happened?" He asked tentatively.

Blaine sighed, biding his time, wondering how to explain how he'd fucked up his relationship so royally.

"I guess the short answer is she never trusted me. I was open with her about my sexuality from the moment we met, and she claimed to be okay with it. In hindsight, she probably never was and I was too blind to see it. Hayden says she hated him and thought – and that's a direct quote – we started fucking the moment she turned her back on us. In the end of the day, we both made mistakes and hurt each other, said things we regretted, and everything fell apart around us."

Liam hummed, his body boneless in Blaine's arms, his breathing slow and steady as he started drifting off.

"Thanks for telling me," he said, his words slurring sleepily. "Do you think..." he began, but paused, the darkness in the room and the quiet of dawn probably making him say things he wouldn't in the light of day. Licking his lips, Liam tried again. "Do you think we'd have ended up here if we were in London?" Blaine frowned, confused. "Here, as in bed," Liam clarified, brushing a gentle kiss on Blaine's collarbone.

"Why do you ask?" Blaine asked cautiously, not sure what answer Liam was looking for. In his mind, it was undoubtedly yes, but he didn't know if saying that out loud would do more damage than good.

Liam lifted a shoulder in a casual shrug. "I was just wondering."

"Does it matter? We're here now."

"No," he said, snuggling closer and kissing Blaine's neck, before yawning. "I love listening to your voice. Tell me a story."

Blaine smiled, kissed the top of Liam's head, and began telling the story of a faraway kingdom, where a lonely king ruled the land until he got snatched by a dragon. Liam started snoring quietly before Blaine got to the end, and just as well because Blaine had no idea how the story ended.

Chapter eleven

Liam watched as Blaine got out of the water, the foamy waves crashing behind him as he ran a hand through his wet hair, the muscles on his arm flexing. He stalked towards Liam, his body so elegant, so fucking *hot*, that Liam's throat felt dry. He swallowed a few times to try and lubricate his vocal cords, then on an instinct reached for his camera. As Blaine neared he snapped a few photos of him, not even looking through the lens. Blaine's blue eyes danced with mischief when he stood right in front of Liam, raising an eyebrow.

"Did you get a good shot or do you want a slow motion replay?"

"Yes, please" Liam said with a grin, aiming the camera back at Blaine and snapping a quick shot.

In his head the whole thing had indeed happened in slow motion. He could still see Blaine's abs flexing as he moved, the water droplets glistening on his skin as they slid down, the smirk Blaine aimed his way when Liam took the first photo.

Blaine shook his head over Liam, cold drops raining on his skin. He squeaked, shielding his camera and storing it safely back in the bag. Unapologetic, Blaine lay on his towel next to Liam.

"Why don't you come with me for a swim next time?" He asked, reaching for the bag and taking out the sun lotion.

"It's cold." Liam shivered remembering the icy cold water when he'd dipped his toes this morning.

"It's fine once you get used to it." Blaine spread sun lotion over his chest and arms, then handed it to Liam as he turned on his belly.

Liam made a non committal sound as he knelt next to Blaine and poured some lotion onto his back. Blaine gave a satisfied moan when Liam started massaging his shoulders, then down his back, careful not to miss a spot. Blaine's trunks had ridden down his hips revealing a sliver of white skin. Heat pooled in Liam's stomach as he noticed the tan line, images of Blaine naked and spread on the bed, his white ass in stark contrast with his tanned skin flooding his mind.

The last time he'd seen Blaine naked his tan was barely visible, and this morning it'd been too dark in the room to take a good look. This new development made Liam's cock rise to attention, and he silently thanked his lucky stars that he'd chosen to wear the loose black shorts instead of his tight trunks today.

Liam's finger traced the tan line on Blaine's lower back, watching as goosebumps appeared under his touch. Blaine stirred, and when Liam looked at him he was biting his lip, his eyes dark under hooded lids.

"If you don't stop touching me we'd have to cut this wonderful day at the beach short," he said, his low voice making Liam shiver despite the heat.

"Oh?" He asked innocently, his eyes widening as if he had no idea what he was doing to Blaine. His hands kept massaging his skin even though the sun lotion had long been absorbed.

"I'm seconds away from humping the towel, babe," Blaine growled, his arm shooting out to catch Liam's wrist. "Either stop touching me or get ready to get thrown over my shoulder and carried to the hotel."

Liam laughed. "How very caveman of you." He shook Blaine's hand off and turned to lie down on his belly next to him. "Is it wrong that I find that kinda hot?" He waggled his eyebrows theatrically.

"Not at all. It works in my favour, actually."

Liam couldn't help but notice how Blaine's eyes twinkled as he watched him, something else hiding behind the humour. He couldn't quite put his finger on it, but it unnerved him. His thoughts drifted to this morning and how Blaine'd held him as they talked. And then indulged him with a made-up story that had lulled him to sleep.

The humour disappeared in Blaine's eyes and he gazed at Liam as if he could read his mind, as if his own thoughts had gone to the early hours of the morning. The intensity in his stare made Liam avert his eyes, looking for refuge anywhere else.

"How about a cocktail?" He said, propping himself up on his elbows and jerking his chin towards the beach bar.

Blaine agreed it was about time to get their first cocktail of the day and they quickly collected their things, and headed for the bar. The guy behind the counter greeted them warmly, his English only slightly accented as he asked for their order.

"Caipirinha for me, please," Liam said, perching on the high stool and dropping his bag at his feet. Blaine took the seat next to him and ordered the same.

The barman's eyes lit up. "You have got to try the new recipe I'm trying out," he said, hands flying dramatically.

He was a small guy, his body lithe and elegant, barely covered in a see-through tank top. His dark skin, smooth and entirely hairless, glowed as if religiously moisturised every day.

"Sure," Liam said, smiling at him.

That was all it took. The guy introduced himself as Diego, talking non-stop as he made their drinks. Liam bit his lip to suppress his grin when Blaine stared at Diego, bewildered, probably wondering why a guy they'd just met was telling them, in great detail, a childhood story that inspired this new cocktail recipe.

"There you go," Diego said, placing the two caipirinhas in front of them with a flourish.

Both Liam and Blaine reached for their glasses at the same time, taking a sip through the short straws under Diego's watchful stare.

"So?" He asked eagerly, his eyes wide and hopeful.

"Um..." Blaine began, glancing at Liam, who hid his grin behind his glass and left him to deal with Diego on his own. "It's really good."

That wasn't enough for Diego. His dark gaze never wavered as he made a 'go on' motion with his hand, still watching Blaine expectantly. Taking another sip, Blaine rolled the liquid around in his mouth and looked upward. Liam wasn't sure if he was stalling, trying to come up with a response that would satisfy Diego, or if he was praying to be hit by lighting right this second. Probably a bit of both.

"It tastes different," Blaine finally said. "There's a salty tang that hits you right from the start, but then dissolves into something sweeter. The fizzy bubbles are a nice touch..." Blaine trailed off, turning to Liam again, the desperate plea in his eyes making him laugh.

Liam placed his glass on the counter, claiming Diego's attention. The barman raised an eyebrow at him, as if challenging him to do better than his friend.

"It tastes like Rio," Liam said, and for some reason that made him a bit sad. Who was going to make him cocktails that tasted like Rio when they were gone in a few days? "It's sweet and bitter at the same time, but it's still beautiful and kinda addictive. I haven't finished this one and I'm already thinking of ordering another one."

Diego seemed satisfied with his answer, if his wide toothy grin was any indication.

"Well done, *amigo*, that was exactly what I was going for." Diego leaned on his elbows on the counter, moving closer to Liam as if to whisper something conspiratorially. Liam met him half way, his head turning a little to the side as he listened to Diego, but his eyes held Blaine's who was watching them with a frown. "But be careful," Diego whispered. "A sip of Rio is all it takes. You may never want to leave."

Liam gasped, Diego's words touching a delicate string inside his soul. Blaine must have sensed Liam's distress because he moved closer, his hand coming to rest on top of Liam's on the counter. He entwined their fingers in silent support while Liam managed to get his bearings.

Diego laughed, leaning away, and Liam felt like the spell was broken. He squeezed Blaine's hand before pulling away to take another sip of his cocktail. As expected, Diego kept chatting as he served everyone, switching from Portuguese to English effortlessly, shaking his hips to the music as he made cocktails and opened beer bottles. The music got louder as the sun started to descent behind the horizon, and soon Liam's stomach growled. They had to go get something to eat – drinking on an empty stomach was a bad idea. Liam didn't want to spend any of his precious remaining days in Rio curled in bed with a hangover.

"Let's go get something to eat," Liam said to Blaine, sliding out of the stool.

Blaine nodded, took one last sip of his drink and pushed the glass away. Diego noticed them leaving and sauntered to them, pouting.

"You guys leaving already? But the party is just starting!" His pout transformed into a flirty grin as he winked at Liam. Apparently, not drinking on the job wasn't a rule Diego followed too closely. The guy had obviously knocked down a few drinks since he'd last served them.

Blaine stepped closer to Liam, bending to take the bag from the floor, then casually wrapping an arm around Liam's shoulders. Diego's eyes moved from Liam to Blaine, but he didn't seem too put off by Blaine's non too subtle 'back off' vibe. Liam had enough of a buzz from his tasty Rio drinks to find that funny, a giggle escaping his mouth before he could stop it.

"You'll be back tomorrow, right?" Diego said, leaning over the counter with a leer. "I see you sitting all on your own every day, while your boyfriend plays with the waves." Diego pointed an elegant finger at Liam. "Next time come and sit here, the first caipirinha is on me." Diego winked again, propping his chin on his palm and licking his lips.

Liam had to smile. The guy was obviously baiting Blaine, for whatever reason, and it seemed to be working. Liam could feel Blaine stiffening beside him, his hand on Liam's shoulder tightening to a point of discomfort. And then there was the low sound Blaine made deep in his throat that sounded suspiciously like growling.

"All right, Diego, cut it off," Liam said, biting his lip to stop his grin from spreading.

Diego blinked innocently, but nobody was fooled. They said their goodbyes and turned to leave when Liam heard Diego call his name. He was waving at them holding some sort of a colourful leaflet.

"I nearly forgot," he said, sneaking out from behind the bar and walking to them. "There's an 80s themed charity race tomorrow night," he said, handing Blaine the brochure. "You should come. It'll be fun. There's a twenty reals registration fee and all of it goes to a LGBT charity called Gêmeos. They do great work here in Brazil but, unfortunately, are very much underfunded with no support from the government." Diego was serious for the first time this evening, his eyes growing even darker, the shadows behind them hinting of a difficult past. "Anyway," he waved a hand in front of him as if to disperse the unpleasant thoughts that had shown on his face. "It's a very popular event and people who race usually promote it on Facebook and Instagram and whatnot, and ask for donations. I'm pretty sure this race, and another event we usually do around Christmas, are the only things keeping Gêmeos afloat."

Liam glanced at Blaine who was reading the colourful brochure with a blank expression. He wasn't sure if it was something Blaine would like to do, but it seemed like a lot of fun to Liam, with the bonus of supporting a great cause.

"Look," Diego said, claiming Liam's attention back. "I'm not trying to guilt trip you into doing this. But I promise you it'll be fun. We all dress up, and there's music, and food and it's a great way to meet people."

Liam looked at Blaine hopefully. He really wanted to do this, but wasn't too keen on going alone.

"It starts at 10 PM?" Blaine asked, raising his eyes from the leaflet for the first time.

"Yeah," Diego said, aiming a charming smile at Blaine. "You interested?"

Before Liam could open his mouth to say they'll think about it, Blaine said, "We'll be there." He was talking to Diego, but was looking at Liam, a smile playing on his lips.

Diego squealed and threw himself at Blaine for a hug, catching him off guard. Blaine patted him awkwardly on the back, but he was still smiling. Diego stepped away to give Liam a hug, too, a longer one, his hand sliding down Liam's back. Before it could reach his ass Blaine slapped it away. Diego giggled playfully, raising his hands in surrender when he let go of Liam.

Blaine shook his head as he watched Diego strut back to the bar. He pulled Liam closer, stirring them in the direction of the hotel.

"I like it when you're jealous," Liam whispered, leaning in closer to Blaine's ear.

"Yeah?"

"Mhm. It's hot." Liam kissed Blaine's cheek, enjoying the roughness of Blaine's jaw. "I didn't even know I'm a sucker for the whole caveman thing, but I'm so turned on right now."

Nothing like a little Dutch courage to make you say the things you were dying to say, but would regret in the morning, right?

"Caveman, eh?" Blaine said and Liam could definitely hear a smile in his voice.

Before he knew what was happening, Blaine had hoisted him up over his shoulder, slapping his ass as he continued to walk as if Liam weighed nothing.

"Put me down, you twat!" Liam shouted, but couldn't help the laughter. "You're such an asshole! Put me the fuck down!"

Blaine slapped his ass cheek again, hard, and Liam felt his cock grow harder even in the uncomfortable position of hanging upside down.

"Me Tarzan. You John. We go cave," Blaine said in a gruff voice.

Liam laughed so hard he thought he might throw up.

"John? Really?" He managed to say.

Blaine stopped, lowering him back to the ground, and Liam realised they were on the sidewalk across from the hotel.

"You haven't seen that new Tarzan gay porn parody?" Blaine asked, his eyes wide with shock.

"No!"

"Oh, baby, I have something really special in store for you tonight."

Liam had believed Diego when he'd said the run would be fun. What he hadn't anticipated was that the preparation for the event would turn out to be just as entertaining. He and Blaine woke up early and went for a run on the deserted beach. The only people there besides them were a group of men jogging at a steady pace, singing some sort of a motivational song. They were all shirtless, wearing black shorts with *bombeiros* written in red letters on the back.

Both Liam and Blaine ogled them as they ran behind them, staring as the muscles on their broad backs rippled with every move.

"What the hell is *bombeiros*? Male strippers?" Blaine said breathlessly.

Trying to keep up with the hot guys in front of them was not easy, but the round, perfectly shaped asses snugly covered with thin black shorts were motivation enough to keep going.

"I don't know," Liam said, panting. "But if we don't stop we won't be able to run for five yards, let alone five kilometres tonight."

They slowed down to a slow jog, watching as the *bombeiros* sped up ahead, their chants still echoing in the quiet of the early morning. When they were merely a dot in the distance, Liam stopped, bracing his hands on his knees as he tried to catch his breath. Blaine joined him, out of breath too, but much more collected. He had his phone out and was tapping on the screen with great concentration.

"Firefighters," he said with glee, tucking his phone back in his pocket.

Liam groaned, every firefighter fantasy he'd ever had finding its way to the front of his mind.

"You sure you don't want to try and catch up?" Blaine asked, laughing when Liam threw him a glare.

"No, but we're running on the beach every morning from now on," he said, delighted when it was Blaine's turn to glare at him.

They spent the rest of the day wandering around Rio Sul shopping centre, looking for 80s inspired clothes and accessories. Liam couldn't remember the last time he'd laughed so much. Watching Blaine try on neon leggings that left little to the imagination, tight shorts that barely covered his ass, and cropped t-shirts in all colours of the rainbow was very amusing. At one point he thought they were going to get thrown out of the shop as Blaine pranced around in a tight crop top, cut off leggings, and knee high socks. But what made Liam drop to the floor of the fitting room in a fit of hysterical laughter was the long blonde Jane Fonda style wig he was proudly flicking from side to side.

Liam tried a few outfits as well, and it was Blaine's turn to laugh at him. But there was also a barely concealed glint of desire in his eyes when Liam put on a pair of bright yellow hot pants and a vest in the same colour, leaving it open at the front and not bothering with a t-shirt underneath. When Liam was finished in the fitting room, Blaine took all the clothes he'd tried on and stuffed them in their shopping basket, ignoring Liam's protests that he hadn't actually decided which ones to get.

"We're buying them all," Blaine said, a low growl in his voice. "And you're going to try them on for me when we get to the hotel. I'll help you choose."

Liam grinned, liking the idea very much. He couldn't wait to get back to their room.

"How about this?" Liam said, stepping out on the balcony.

Blaine's eyes roamed over his body, greedily taking in the view. Liam spun around, curving his spine, thrusting his ass out, making sure Blaine saw exactly how short these shorts were.

"The leg warmers are a nice touch, don't you think?" He asked, looking over his shoulder at Blaine.

He had no time to react before Blaine crowded him against the door, his arm circling Liam's waist and pressing him back against Blaine's chest.

"Not bad," Blaine said, nipping at Liam's earlobe.

"Not bad?" Liam would have argued that the outfit was amazing, sexy and fun, but Blaine slid a hand over the thin fabric of the shorts and squeezed Liam's already hard dick. Liam forgot how to speak.

Dropping his head on Blaine's shoulder, Liam watched their reflection in the glass doors as Blaine rubbed his dick through the shorts. The slow, smooth touch was driving him crazy with need, and he needed more, so much more.

"Baby?" Liam said, the word coming out as a husky whisper.

"Hm?" Blaine murmured, his eyes meeting Liam's in their reflection in the window. His hand kept stroking, moving all so slow, the friction of the soft fabric making Liam crave a harder, faster touch.

"I want you to fuck me," Liam said, bucking his hips into Blaine's hand.

Blaine stilled for a second, then pressed his palm harder against Liam's cock. Liam moaned, his knees melting, bright light exploding behind his lids. His cock was leaking, making the front of his shorts wet, and he was moments away from coming.

Turning sharply in Blaine's arms, Liam grabbed his hips and pulled him closer, mashing their erections together. He kissed him, grinding against him, mindless with lust and anticipation.

"Let's go inside," Blaine said between kisses.

"No," Liam pulled away, walking backwards to the hammock. When his knees hit the fabric, he turned and lay on it, spreading his legs and fisting his cock through the shorts.

"Fuck," Blaine swore, closing his eyes. "Is that thing going to hold us both?"

Liam lifted his hips off the hammock, then slammed back down, looking at Blaine with a playful smirk.

"Looks pretty sturdy to me," he said, bouncing on it some more. When Blaine stood frozen on the spot, his gaze locked on Liam, he added, "Are you going to go get the condoms and lube, or shall I start without you?" He wiggled out of his shorts to emphasise his point, his cock jumping eagerly out.

Blaine dashed inside, and while waiting, Liam took off the rest of his clothes, throwing them on the floor. He wrapped a hand around his shaft, stroking leisurely, not trying to get himself off, but simply enjoying the soft pressure.

He'd wanted Blaine to fuck him ever since they'd met. He'd never felt such strong attraction towards another man, the fantasy of what it would be like playing on a loop in his mind every time he'd jerked off.

"I thought you weren't going to start without me?" Blaine's voice anchored him to the present, and Liam turned to see Blaine stepping out on the balcony. A very naked, very sexy Blaine, walking towards him with predatory intent that made him shiver with anticipation.

He stopped right next to the hammock, his cock hard and beautiful, and right in Liam's face. He couldn't resist a little taste, scooting a little closer and wrapping his lips around the head.

Blaine cursed, then moaned loudly, burying his hands in Liam's hair. For a fleeting moment Liam wondered if someone could see them, but their balcony was tucked away in an alcove, and they were on the fifth floor, so chances were they were pretty well hidden from view. They could definitely be heard, though, and Liam found that the thought of someone listening in as they fucked excited him.

He moaned around Blaine's cock, sucking him in deeper, letting Blaine guide his head, whimpering when Blaine pulled away.

“Scoot,” Blaine said, sliding down next to Liam.

It was tight fit, but the hammock didn’t budge under their combined weight.

“How do you want it, baby?” Blaine asked, running a hand through Liam’s hair and cupping the back of his neck. He didn't wait for a response before he claimed Liam’s mouth in an urgent, needy kiss that left Liam a helpless, whimpering mess in his arms. He was so close to coming and they hadn’t even started yet.

Their lips kept moving against each other, tongues exploring, hands caressing every part of their bodies they could reach. There was a certain urgency to their touches, but no haste. Liam wanted to enjoy this for as long as possible, even if he spontaneously combusted along the way.

“Turn around,” Blaine whispered against his lips, and Liam complied without a second thought.

He was drunk on Blaine, on Rio, on desire and lust and need, and he’d do anything Blaine told him to.

With a little careful manoeuvring, Liam turned, his back pressed against Blaine’s chest. Blaine snuck his arm under Liam’s head, while his mouth explored Liam’s neck, his jaw, his shoulder, nipping and licking at his skin until Liam’s bones turned to liquid. He curled his fingers around his cock, unable to resist the urge to stoke himself. It was all too much, too much sensation, too much feeling. He needed something to release all that pressure inside him, make him explode.

Blaine gently pushed on Liam's thigh until it fell forward, spreading Liam's legs wider. Liam gasped as Blaine's slick finger found his hole, rubbing and massaging it, getting it ready for his cock. Liam shivered at the thought, the hand on his shaft speeding up, his breaths coming out in desperate pants.

"Slow down," Blaine whispered in his ear, breathing hard. "I want you to come when I'm inside you."

Liam whimpered, slowing down his pace with Herculean effort. Instinct had taken over all his senses, turning him into a body of need and desire, not letting any conscious thought into his fogged brain.

Blaine's slick finger entered him, making Liam snap back to reality.

"Fuck, Blaine," he said in a husky voice. "Warn a guy."

Blaine chuckled, kissed Liam's neck and added a second finger. Liam squirmed, not really enjoying the sensation. He loved being fucked, but the preparation annoyed him more than anything.

"I don't really like fingers," he said, pulling away from Blaine while turning to look at him over his shoulder.

Blaine removed his hand, wrapped it around Liam's waist and leaned in to kiss him. Liam's erection had wilted a bit, but Blaine's lips brought it back to life. He gasped when Blaine reached for his cock, entwining their fingers as they both stroked up and down Liam's shaft. All too soon Blaine broke their kiss, his fingers around Liam's cock disappearing as he made quick work of the condom. Liam bit his lip in anticipation, pushing his ass out to meet Blaine's cock.

Blaine laughed, the sound low and deep, and full of wicked promises.

"Get on with it, Blaine," Liam said, with an exasperated huff.

"So impatient," Blaine tisked. "So eager," his voice dropped even lower. "So hot for me."

Liam had a witty comeback on the tip of his tongue, but then Blaine was pushing into him in one long, slow motion, and Liam forgot all the words in his vocabulary.

"You okay?" Blaine asked, his voice strained as if he was barely controlling himself to keep still.

Liam tried to speak but only a croaked sound came out. The burn of Blaine's cock inside him was wearing off and he needed him to start moving before he lost his mind.

"Move," Liam managed to say, throwing his arm back around Blaine's waist and pulling him closer, as if that was possible.

Blaine moved slowly a few times, making Liam's eyes roll back in his head. God, this felt so good. He'd missed this, missed it so much that when Blaine started thrusting his hips faster, harder, oh God, *harder*, Liam's orgasm erupted in a flash of white lights and colourful fireworks, and all the fucking stars all at once.

He couldn't catch his breath, couldn’t move, couldn’t do anything but float as the pleasure overtook his entire world. The hammock bounced in rhythm with Blaine’s thrusts, his moans growing louder, his breathing more laboured, his teeth on Liam's skin leaving angry red marks, he was sure of it, but all he could do was whimper, and push back against Blaine, and tremble when a second wave of pleasure, sharper than the first, rolled through his entire body.

Liam didn’t know how long they lay there in the hammock, under the darkening sky, listening to the waves and their own panting breaths. He didn't know how long it had been before Blaine’s softening cock slipped out of him, or Blaine wrapped him in his arms and kissed him, murmuring soft words Liam didn't understand. All he knew was that he'd never in his entire life felt as peaceful as he did right now. He had everything he’d ever wanted, and he was happy.

Chapter twelve

Blaine startled awake by loud music coming from the beach. Liam was still snoring softly in his arms, and Blaine didn't want to wake him, but a nagging feeling at the back of his mind insisted there was something important they had to do. Lifting his head to look over the balcony railing, Blaine saw the beach was swarmed with people, lights, and rainbow decorations.

"Shit!" He swore, pushing at Liam's shoulder. "Liam," he said, shaking him a little. Liam murmured something but didn't open his eyes. "Liam, baby, we have to go right now or we'll be late for the fucking charity run."

"What?" Liam said, confused, opening his eyes and yawning.

"Babe, we have to go, now."

Blaine swung his feet over the edge of the hammock, careful not to turn it over and dump Liam onto the floor. His movements were jerky enough to jostle Liam awake. Blaine watched as his eyes widened, turned to look at the beach over his shoulder, then hopped off the hammock, nearly falling on his face.

What followed was a whirlwind of the quickest shared shower ever – no touching or even looking at one another allowed – a frantic gathering of clothes, tearing labels off and hastily putting them on, without even sparing a glance in the mirror. Liam fixed Blaine's knee high socks while Blaine pointed out Liam's t-shirt was on backwards. They helped each other with the glow in the dark accessories, tied knots, secured bracelets and straightened their clothes, making sure they looked presentable.

There was no time for any doubts. The door slammed behind them as they ran along the corridor and then down the stairs – there was no time to wait for the lift – and then crossed the road in a flurry of neon coloured clothes. They made it to the race starting point with ten minutes to spare, out of breath but grinning like idiots.

"Hey! You made it!" Diego said the moment he spotted them. He waved them over to a small table with a big 'Registration' sign on it. His see-through pink t-shirt left little to the imagination, and Blaine found himself fixated on Diego's nipple piercings. "You pulled that off in a day? I'm impressed," he flirted, his eyes stripping Liam naked.

Liam blushed and it was visible even in the artificial glow of the lights spread all around them.

"Thanks," Liam said, tucking his hands in his minuscule shorts. The same shorts that had driven Blaine mad with lust that same afternoon.

The memory of fucking Liam on the hammock, making him incoherent with pleasure as he moved inside him, sent jolts of desire through Blaine's body, his cock stiffening in his own shorts. He had to stop thinking about Liam, moaning in his arms, his body trembling as he came, his skin flushed and damp...

"Well, I see someone is *really* excited to be here," Diego said, his voice pulling Blaine out of his x-rated thoughts.

Blaine threw him a glare, adjusting his cock in the thin, neon green shorts while Diego watched his every move, not even remotely embarrassed to be blatantly staring at another guy's crotch. Liam snorted, and Blaine glared at him too, but the guy only smirked at him, then proceeded to bend over the table, push his delicious ass out, and fill the registration form for both of them.

For fuck's sake. It was going to be a long night. A long, uncomfortable night where Blaine would have to run five kilometres with a hard on. Great.

"Hey, Diego?" Liam said, taking out his phone from the pink bum bag he was wearing. "Would you mind taking a couple of pictures of us? We'd like to post them online and promote the event, maybe get a few donations."

"Sure," Diego purred, coming round the table and taking Liam's phone. His bright yellow leggings hugged every single muscle on his legs and ass, shimmering as he moved, and for some reason he didn't look weird wearing a pink cropped top, yellow leggings, and neon green armbands.

The first photo was a bit awkward, Liam standing next to Blaine, not sure what to do. Diego rolled his eyes and encouraged them to give him some energy, some charisma for God's sake, and Blaine took over. He wrapped his arms around Liam, positioning him in front of him, resting his chin on Liam's shoulder. Diego approved, and motioned for them to keep going. Liam turned in Blaine's arms and smiled, his golden eyes catching the twinkling lights all around them. Blaine dipped him down, making him squeak in surprise, but he quickly got on with the idea and wrapped a leg around Blaine's hips. Blaine kissed him in the classic pose, smiling as he did so when Diego shouted words of encouragement.

They took a few more shots and were really getting into the impromptu photo session when Diego waltzed over to them and gave Liam his phone back. The screen was still lit and Blaine couldn't help but notice it wasn't the camera app that was active. It was the phone book, and Diego's name, plus a little heart eyes emoticon, was right on top.

"You've got to be fucking kidding me," Blaine said, glowering at Diego.

The bastard simply winked at him, shrugged, and ran off to the small stage where the race would start.

"Come on, caveman," Liam said, grabbing his hand, and barely keeping his smile at bay. "Let's go line up."

Blaine scowled at him and had the sudden urge to throw him over his shoulder again. Instead, he smacked his ass, hard, wiping the smirk off Liam's face.

They lined up behind the stage, joining the rest of the participants. Blaine hadn't really thought about the scale of the event, but judging by the huge crowd, it was really popular. Everywhere he turned he was blinded by neon coloured clothes, glow in the dark accessories, and bad 80s wigs. The crowd was also quite eclectic, ranging from young gay couples to older men and women of all nationalities. Blaine could hear lots of different languages spoken all around them.

What everyone had in common, apart from the 80s inspired attire, was that they were all smiling, enthusiastically waving their hands and trying to talk to each other even if they didn't speak the same language. The joyful atmosphere was contagious and Blaine soon found himself relaxing, wiping the memory of Diego's number in Liam's phone. Well, not wiping per se, but putting it on the back burner for now.

"Ladies and gentlemen, and everyone in between," Diego said, grabbing the attention of the crowd. Everyone cheered and turned to the stage. "Welcome to the annual Gêmeos charity race!" The crowd cheered again, the noise deafening. Liam whistled loudly right next to Blaine, startling him. "Thank you so much for being here tonight, and for your generous donations. You have no idea how much this all helps in our fight against prejudice, homelessness, sickness, addiction, and everything else LGBT people here in Brazil face every single day. It is because of your support and generosity that Gêmeos is still standing, still proudly fighting for equality and quietly supporting those who need it." More cheers followed, then Diego raised his hands to quiet everyone down. "Tonight, just like every year, we race from Posto 8," he pointed at the tall post at the other side of the beach, "to Posto 12 and back. The after party will be right here when everyone has crossed the finish line. Good luck, everyone!"

The crowd clapped and whistled, as Diego beamed proudly from the stage. He quickly repeated his speech in Portuguese and Spanish, apologising he didn't know any more languages. While he was still talking, Liam took out his phone and Blaine couldn't help his curiosity, peaking at the screen over his shoulder.

He was hoping Liam would delete Diego's number, but instead he pulled up the gallery and scrolled through their photos from tonight. Glancing at Blaine over his shoulder, Liam smiled and pointed at the picture currently on the screen. It was the one that Blaine had dipped him down and kissed him, and it was amazing. Blaine couldn't stop staring at the curve of Liam's ass in the barely-there shorts and his lean muscles as he held on to Blaine.

Liam tapped on the screen a few times and uploaded the photo to all his social media accounts, quickly typing in the details of the charity and promising more photos if people donated. Blaine had left his phone at the hotel, so Liam tagged him so that his followers could see it, too.

The race went smoothly considering the amount of people taking part. The whole stretch of the run was lit up by scattered portable lights in all colours of the rainbow, people cheering the participants on and giving away bottles of water and energy bars. It was only five kilometres, but most of the runners were obviously inexperienced, stopping for a rest every few hundred metres.

Liam and Blaine adopted a slow, but steady pace, and before long they were circling Posto 12 and going back. Liam didn't seem to be able to stop smiling, talking to people as they passed by, his eyes absorbing every little detail.

"I wish I had my camera with me," Liam said, a little breathless.

"That would have been pretty uncomfortable," Blaine said, imagining Liam running on the beach with that monster of a camera around his neck.

Liam nodded, slowed down a bit before taking out his phone. He still managed to snap a few photos during the race even if it wasn't with his hi-tech camera.

At the finish line, everyone was greeted by an enthusiastic crowd and given a plastic medal. Liam took a few selfies of them with their medals, ignoring

Blaine's protests that they were sweaty and gross. He used some sort of filter while taking the pictures that made their eyes twinkle and their skin looked flushed rather than sweaty. After he was satisfied with their selfies, he took pictures of other people crossing the finish line, some even posed for him. It all went on social media, reminding people to donate to Gêmeos if they could.

"Blaine!" Liam exclaimed, a bit too loudly considering Blaine was standing right next to him. "Look!" He turned the phone screen to him and Blaine saw the picture he'd posted before the race had over a thousand likes already.

"Wow, that's impressive," Blaine said, taking the phone from Liam and scrolling through the comments.

Lots of people had commented they'd donated, some even mentioned they'd taken part in the previous races.

"And there's like two hundred retweets on Twitter, and lots of likes and comments on Facebook," Liam said, taking his phone back and tucking it back in his bum bag.

Blaine pulled him in his arms and kissed him, unable to resist Liam's charm any longer. When Liam was that excited about something there was this aura around him that drew people in. Or maybe it was just Blaine. It didn't matter. Liam was gorgeous, and kind, and funny and so sexy, and right now he was Blaine's.

A flash went off somewhere in Blaine peripheral vision and they both turned to see Diego snapping a picture of them as they kissed. He winked at them when they turned to look at him, and sauntered away.

"Look for it on Facebook and my blog," he called over his shoulder.

Blaine knew he would. He really wanted that photo.

The next morning Blaine woke up sore as hell. Also, alone in the bed. He groaned when he heard the shower running, knowing that if Liam was up so early and already getting ready, they were going to do *stuff* today.

Rubbing a hand over his face, Blaine sat in the bed, yawning several times in quick succession. Every muscle in his body ached as he moved. After the run yesterday, they'd stayed at the party for a few hours, dancing and drinking, talking to random people and exchanging contact details. Blaine had lost count how many pictures Liam had posted on social media, but from what he'd seen before they turned in for the night, the event was generating a lot of interest. And so were Liam and Blaine. There was a hashtag with their names on Twitter, and Blaine blushed when he recalled the things he'd seen on Tumblr.

He needed to check his own accounts and emails but he couldn't be bothered. Liam was naked and soapy in the bathroom, and Blaine wanted to forget about social media and the internet for a while. As a radio DJ it was all a part of his job, but he was on holiday with a guy he really liked, and their days together were quickly running out.

With newly-found strength, Blaine got out of bed and headed for the bathroom, already imagining all the things he'd do to Liam in there.

Blaine had been a bit worried when Liam told him they were going on a *favela* tour. He'd read numerous articles about how dangerous it was to visit the *favelas*, and couldn't help but wonder why they needed to do it at all. But Liam had assured him it was perfectly safe when they were with an organised tour, so here they were, in a ten year old blue van, with twelve other people, driving up the narrow cobble stoned streets towards their first stop.

Their tour guide, Rafael, was a young man with shoulder length dark hair and soulful dark eyes framed by the longest lashes Blaine'd ever seen. He sat in the seat next to the driver, facing the passengers and talked about the history of the *favelas* in an accented but very fluent English. Liam listened carefully, even asking some questions, but Blaine focused on looking out the window.

This was the unglamorous part of Rio. The part which tourists rarely saw. But it was still part of this amazing city and had shaped its history throughout the years. Blaine listened to Rafael speak, noting down details like the fact that there were over a thousand *favelas* in Brazil, and over twenty percent of Rio's over six million population lived there. But his attention was focused on the views outside, the brightly coloured houses with potted flowers on the windows, hanging laundry and peeling paint. The elaborate network of electric cables haphazardly dangling over the streets. The artistic graffiti painted over the walls. The people walking around or standing in groups, chatting and laughing.

Finally, they arrived at their first scheduled stop – the largest *favela* in Rio de Janeiro, Rocinha. Rafael warned them not to take pictures inside people's houses, even if they were invited in. The people of Rocinha had been welcoming tourists for years, but still, this was their home and should be treated with respect.

Blaine looked at Liam and saw his own frown mirrored on Liam's face.

"What kind of people come on these tours if the guide has to actually say that? Isn't it common sense?" Liam said, shaking his head.

Blaine agreed with a nod and followed the last of their group as they piled off the van. Rafael took them on a walk around the *favela*, pointing out details like art on the walls, little stalls with hand-made jewellery for sale, as well as local vendors selling popular Brazilian street food. He told the group they could wander around on their own and meet by the van in about half an hour.

Liam already had his camera out and was taking pictures of everything that caught his eye. Blaine snapped a few shots on his phone as they walked, too, but he mainly looked around, trying to get a sense of the place. He didn't feel threatened in any way, each and every native they passed nodded at them and smiled. There was no sense of despair as Blaine'd expected, rather a sense of a close knit community who did their best to survive. There was poverty, sure, it was evident everywhere around them, but no misery.

When they reached the end of the street, a view opened in front of them that took Blaine's breath away. The whole of Rio was displayed beneath of them, the cerulean water of the ocean glittering in the sun like a million sapphires. He could see everything – the beaches, the apartment buildings, the hills and forests, all proudly watched over by Christ the Redeemer.

It was beautiful and magical and just a little intimidating.

"It's perfect," Liam said, his face hidden behind the camera as he took photo after photo of the gorgeous view. "Isn't it?" He added when Blaine didn't immediately respond.

"Yeah. It is." Blaine stared into Liam's eyes, wanting to tell him so many things. He wanted to say them right now, in the light of day, with all of Rio as his witness, because he felt them all the time, not just in the throes of passion or the safe darkness of the night.

"Liam..." he began, but paused when Liam's eyes skimmed past his face and over his shoulder to something behind him.

"You have to be joking," Liam murmured, stomping past Blaine.

Blaine turned, watching as Liam walked up to a couple standing at the threshold of a house, camera clicking loudly.

"Excuse me," Liam said, and they turned to look at him with a scowl. "What do you think you're doing? Rafael explicitly said to respect people's houses and not take any pictures without permission."

The woman opened her mouth to speak but the man squared his shoulders and cut her off.

"The door was open and there's nobody here," the man said in an American accent. He was glaring at Liam, his cheeks reddening, whether with anger or shame Blaine wasn't sure.

He walked up to them, stood behind Liam in show of silent support. Both the man and the woman looked at him but said nothing, focusing back on Liam.

"It's not a big deal. Back off, buddy," the man said, dismissing Liam and turning his back on him.

Liam was vibrating with anger, but thankfully the couple walked away without another word.

"Fucking idiots," Liam murmured. "Entitled bastards."

"Hey," Blaine said softly, pulling Liam in his arms.

Liam hugged him for a moment, but then pulled away, clearly still annoyed.

"It's fine. Let's just go. I think it's time to head back anyway."

He stomped down the street towards the van, and Blaine followed without another word.

The group had already gathered when they arrived and were walking around looking at the stalls with jewellery, knick knacks and souvenirs. Liam headed that way, too, taking pictures of the colourful displays and buying some things as well. Blaine was tired, his muscles still feeling the strain from last night's escapades, so he decided to hang back, sitting on a bench nearby.

All too soon Rafael called everyone back to the van and they headed to their next destination. On the way there, he explained about the importance of education and communal support in the *favelas*, the work some of the local charities did here and how half of the income from ever tour was going to the local schools.

The next stop was at a primary school, and right next to it a community centre called Para Ti. They all piled off the van again, following Rafael into the school and meeting some of the kids and the teachers. They had lunch at the small café in the community centre together with the locals and the kids, who were noisy and happy, and brought so much energy to their group.

Liam asked for permission from one the teachers who spoke decent English to take pictures with the kids, even giving the camera to one of them to take a photo of their entire group. Blaine's heart nearly stopped when the kid held the camera, already seeing it in his mind's eye as it dropped to the floor and crashed into a thousand pieces. He glanced at Liam to see if he was having the same reaction over his expensive camera, but Liam was looking at the kid with a smile, gesturing for him to put the strap around his neck. The little boy did and Blaine could breathe easily again.

"Blaine, come over here," Liam called, waving Blaine over.

Blaine took one last bite of his sandwich, downed his drink, and walked to the group of kids and teachers sitting on the floor. He sat next to Liam who immediately wrapped an arm around his shoulders and gestured for the kid with the camera to keep going.

When it was time to leave, the kids swarmed them, giving them both hugs and talking in rapid Portuguese. Blaine looked helplessly at one of the teachers, hoping to get some sort of translation. She smiled at him and said,

"They hope you'll both come back. They like you."

Blaine grinned, knowing they probably wouldn't see these kids again, but he couldn't say that and crush their precious little smiles, could he?

Liam crouched down next to the boy who still held his camera, carefully extracting it from his grasp, then ruffling his hair. They waved goodbye and joined the rest of their group who were already back in the van.

Their last stop for the day was a small *favela* called Vila Canoas. Rafael told them that while Rocinha was the largest *favela* in Brazil with just under a hundred thousand residents, Vila Canoas housed less than three thousand people.

The atmosphere in Vila Canoas was much more intimate, the hustle and bustle of the main square in Rocinha nowhere to be found. The houses looked pretty much the same, the streets were steep and cobble stoned, and the network of cables running from the electricity posts to the windows and inside the houses hung even more precariously over their heads. They managed to find a spot between two houses with great views over Rio, from a slightly different angle. After what felt like a million photos later, they headed back to the meeting point, led by the faint sound of drums and singing.

Liam looked at Blaine, confused, there hadn't been any music a few minutes ago. Blaine shrugged and they kept walking, rounding a corner to see a couple of young boys, no more than seven or eight, dancing as an older man played some sort of a handheld drum. The boys were laughing and singing as they danced, their moves perfectly synchronised with the beat.

The rest of the group was nowhere to be found, only Rafael smoked a cigarette nearby, leaning back against a wall as he watched them.

Liam raised his camera and pointed at it and then the kids, silently asking the adult behind the drum if he could take any pictures. The man smiled and nodded, and Liam gave him the thumbs up. Just as he started taking pictures of the dancing kids, one of the boys ran up to Blaine, took his hand and led him to the make shift dance floor. Blaine looked around for someone to help him get out of this situation, because he couldn't imagine moving like these kids. He'd look like an ogre next to them; his body wasn't genetically equipped to dance like that.

Liam grinned behind the camera and was no help at all, even motioning for Blaine to get into it as he snapped photo after photo. Blaine scowled at him, but when one of the kids tugged on his arm again, he schooled his features and did the best he could. He danced.

"Samba," the kid said, pointing at Blaine, then moving his arms and legs with elegant grace Blaine could never achieve.

The rhythm seemed to get faster and soon Blaine was out of breath. Thankfully, the rest of their group joined them and they were ready to go.

"That was pretty amazing," Liam said as he walked next to Blaine towards the van. "I didn't know you could move like that, Blaine." He raised an eyebrow at him, smirking.

"Shut up," Blaine grunted, but had to bite the inside of his cheek to stop himself from smiling.

After dinner, they went for a moonlit walk on the beach, holding hands in comfortable silence, kissing and laughing under the twinkling stars. The water was cold, but they played with the little waves anyway, splashing each other and chasing each other knee deep in the water.

"You'll pay for that!" Blaine shouted when Liam kicked at the water, soaking his t-shirt, then ran off laughing his head off.

He chased after him, catching him easily – laughing like a maniac while running was not conductive to developing speed. Liam kept giggling even when Blaine wrapped his hands around his waist, hoisted him up, then plonked him down on the shore. A wave chose that exact moment to crash right into Liam, soaking him wet.

"See? Even the ocean is on my side," Blaine said, grinning, extending a hand to help Liam up.

Liam stood, his clothes wet, his hair plastered around his face, but he was smiling, his cheeks flushed with delight. They kissed right there in the water, the waves playing around their legs, their harsh breaths and soft moans intensifying as the kiss deepened.

"Ow!" Liam suddenly cried out, jumping back and away from Blaine. "Fuck!" He bent down, wrapping a hand around his ankle.

"What's wrong?" Blaine crouched down next to him, looking at the spot Liam was holding the waves around them shielded it from view.

"Something fucking stung me," Liam said, his voice tight with pain.

Blaine helped him up and led him away from the water's reach. Liam sat on the sand, his face distorted in agony.

"Let me see." Blaine leaned over Liam's leg, frowning. The moon was bright and nearly full, and the light coming from it was enough to see the angry red marks right above Liam's ankle.

"Shit," Blaine swore, unzipping his pocket and taking out the hotel keycard. "It was a jellyfish. There're a couple of tentacles still attached." He looked up at Liam whose eyes were wide with shock and fear. "I've done this before, so, trust me?"

Liam nodded, biting his lip. Blaine had to ignore the fear in Liam's eyes, and the need to comfort him, and instead focus on treating the sting. Carefully, he scraped the two tentacles from the skin using the tip of his keycard, double checking to make sure he got them all.

"There," he said, kneeling next to Liam. "I removed the tentacles so no more poison will be released into the skin, but we have to get back to the hotel as soon as possible and wash the wound with vinegar." Liam looked at him uncertainly, wincing as he moved his leg to stand up. "It'll be fine, okay?" Blaine said, helping him up. "Jellyfish stings are common and rarely life threatening. The pain is fucking annoying, but it'll subside once we tend to the wound and get you a few painkillers. You'll be as good as new in a couple of days."

He was talking, supporting a limping Liam around the waist as they walked. Liam didn't say anything, probably focused on not crying out in pain with every step. But Blaine kept talking, trying to set his mind at ease that it would be fine. They'd go to the hospital if the sting looked or felt worse tomorrow morning, but for now they'd do whatever they could to keep Liam as comfortable as possible.

Back at the hotel, the staff were fast to react and incredibly helpful. They brought two bottles of vinegar up to their room, as well as pain killers, bandages, and antibiotic ointment. Blaine tipped them well and set on to treating the sting. Liam was still not saying much, but he cooperated with Blaine's efforts to help, not complaining even when the vinegar wash must have stung like a bitch.

When he was sure the vinegar had done enough to neutralise the poison released from the tentacles, Blaine helped Liam in the shower, the hot water deactivating any leftover effect from the toxins, and relieving the pain. Liam exhaled in relief, dropping his head on Blaine's shoulder as Blaine held him, kissing his temple.

"I think I need to lie down," Liam whispered against Blaine's skin.

Blaine helped him to the bed, bandaging the sting as Liam sat down, careful not to wince at the sight of the bright red wounds. They didn't seem infected or inflamed, but he'd check on them later to make sure Liam wasn't allergic to the venom.

"Take this, just in case." Blaine handed Liam a glass of water and a couple of pain killers to help Liam sleep through the night.

Liam swallowed the pills, then crawled up on the bed, sighing when his head reached the pillow.

Blaine followed, lying down next to him, wanting to take him in his arms, but not sure if it'd be welcome under the circumstances. He reached for his phone on the nightstand instead, googling how to treat jellyfish stings to make sure he'd done everything correctly. He'd done this about five years ago when a friend of his got stung on a beach in Spain during an ill-advised skinny dip in the middle of the night, but it wouldn't hurt to double check.

Liam stirred next to him, turning gingerly and moving to snuggle in Blaine's arms. Laying his head on Blaine's chest, and wrapping an arm around his waist, Liam made a content little noise, his breathing slowing down almost immediately.

Blaine smiled as he looked down at Liam, calm and relaxed, seeking comfort in Blaine's arms. His stomach did a little flip at the thought of Liam seeing him as something more than a holiday fling, but not being ready to admit so yet. They still had a few more days left here, maybe Blaine could make him see that what they had didn't have to end when they got on the plane. He had this crazy idea taking root in his mind about how they could make this last, and how they could make Liam's dreams come true.

But it was scary to voice it out, and even scarier thinking about Liam's reaction. What if he laughed in his face and dismissed it as nothing more than a fantasy?

Blaine sighed, kissing the top of Liam's head as he fiddled with his phone one handed, activating the camera app. He snapped a photo of them, Blaine looking up at the camera while Liam slept peacefully in his arms.

On an impulse, he sent the photo to Hayden, adding underneath,

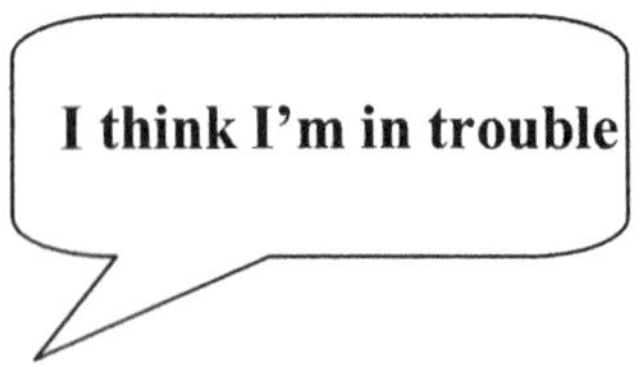

He put a blushing emoticon at the end of the sentence, not that Hayden needed that clarification. He'd get what kind of trouble Blaine meant just by looking at the picture. Even to Blaine's eyes it looked intimate, raw, and way too intense to post on social media.

Hayden replied with a meme of a guy who had pink paper hearts stuck on top of his eyes, with the caption: 'Heart eyes, motherfucker'.

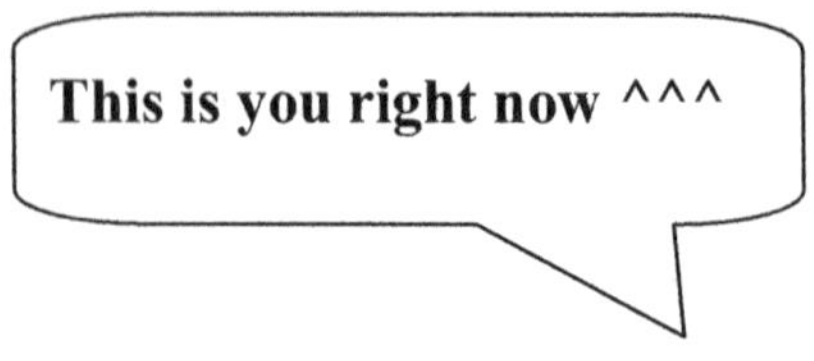

Blaine laughed quietly, shaking his head. He texted back, clutching his phone tightly and eagerly awaiting Hayden's response.

Was it really that easy?

Chapter thirteen

When Liam woke up the next day, his leg felt much better than the night before, but it was still uncomfortable. He didn't want to pout, or make a big deal out of it, especially when Blaine was going out of his way to tend to the sting and make Liam feel better. But, for the first time since they'd arrived in Rio, Liam didn't feel like leaving the hotel room at all. He was afraid of getting sand into the wound if they went to the beach and just wasn't up to doing anything.

His mood was sour, and he didn't want to take it out on Blaine, but it was his fucking birthday and he was stuck in a hotel room with a jellyfish sting throbbing on his leg, and fuck it all, he wanted to curl under the covers, draw the curtains, and be miserable.

"Why don't you go out?" He asked Blaine when he settled on the bed next to him, book in hand.

It was still early morning, but Liam had woken up a while ago, his leg itching and uncomfortable as hell. Blaine didn't have to suffer with him all day, he could go out and do whatever he wanted, Liam didn't need a babysitter.

"We don't have to do everything together," Liam said, unable to hide his irritation.

Blaine regarded him, his expression unreadable.

“I know,” he said, opening his book and settling more comfortably on the bed.

Liam grabbed the book and tossed it on his nightstand.

“I don’t need you here. Go out and have fun. I’ll be fine.” His words were clipped and he glared at Blaine, hoping he’ll get the fucking hint and leave.

Maybe the pain from the sting was getting to him, or the fact that they hadn’t spent more than a few minutes apart for more than a week, but Liam was getting angry at Blaine’s blank expression. It was obvious he was trying to control the way he really felt about all this, and not hurt Liam’s precious feelings, but Liam was not a child and he could take care of himself.

“Fine,” Blaine said, getting up and heading to the wardrobe. “But you call me if you need anything.” He pointedly held out his phone for Liam to see before tucking it in his pocket.

Liam grunted something in agreement, but he knew he wouldn't call. He wanted to be alone and wallow in his own misery for a little while. He was being a dick and he knew it, but he’d apologise later. Right now, all he wanted was another pain killer and sleep.

Liam was asleep before Blaine left the room. He didn't know how long he'd slept, but when he woke up his stomach was cramping with hunger, and he was lightheaded. Blaine was nowhere to be seen, but when Liam looked more closely there was a note on Blaine's pillow.

> Clean the wound when you wake up, and eat something. I'll come pick you up around 7pm. Meet me in front of the hotel.
>
> xx Blaine

Liam was too hungry to feel annoyed. He ordered a sandwich from room service, and headed to the bathroom. Unwrapping the bandage he saw that the sting was much better – still red, but not at all swollen and it seemed to be shrinking in size. He took a quick shower, dried himself off, and spread some of the antibiotic cream over the sting. It was still a bit itchy, but didn't hurt anymore.

The knock came just as Liam was pulling on his sweats, and he opened the door to room service, his stomach growling embarrassingly. The guy carrying his food smiled at him, accepted his tip and left, leaving Liam to devour the sandwich in four bites. His phone rang as he carried his empty plate to the table, and he made a detour to get it from the nightstand.

"Hey," Liam said, seeing Blaine's name on the screen. Tucking his phone between ear and shoulder, he walked to the table and dumped the plate there. "What's up?"

"Are you ready?" Blaine asked, his voice muffled by what sounded like heavy traffic around him.

"For what?"

"Didn't you see my note?"

"Oh, yes, sorry, I did see it, but I kinda forgot about it because I was starving." Liam walked to the bed and reread the note, turning the phone to look at the time. "You want me to meet you outside in fifteen minutes?"

"Make that ten," Blaine said. A loud car horn beeped really close to Blaine and Liam had to pull the phone away from his ear.

"Where the hell are you?"

"I'm on my way," Blaine said, making Liam roll his eyes. Before he could ask any more questions, Blaine said, "Look, I have to go, but make sure you take your phone, and the cream and bandages from the bathroom. Oh, and a hoodie. I'll see you in ten, okay?"

Liam didn't have a chance to respond before the line went dead.

Twelve minutes later he walked out of the hotel lobby to find Blaine waiting outside perched on a parked Vespa. Liam approached him, cautiously eyeing the royal blue scooter.

"What's going on?"

Blaine grinned, pulling him in his arms and kissing him softly on the lips. His gaze searched Liam's, a worry line appearing between his brows.

"You okay? How's the sting?" Blaine asked, looking down at Liam's leg.

"It's much better." Liam paused, lifting his hands to rest them on Blaine's cheeks. "I'm sorry I was an asshole this morning." Blaine opened his mouth to say something, but Liam leaned in and kissed him, silencing whatever he was about to say. "Don't find excuses for me," he said when they pulled apart. "I was a dick and I know it, and I'm sorry."

Blaine nodded, then turned and handed Liam a helmet in the same royal blue shade as the Vespa.

"I have a surprise for you, but I need you to tell me if you're up for it."

"How can I say if I'm up for it if I don't know what it is?" Liam asked, already putting the helmet on. There was no doubt in his mind that he was going to do whatever Blaine wanted them to do, and he was actually pretty excited to see what Blaine'd planned.

"As long as you're not in pain and feel well enough for a little adventure you should be alright." Blaine winked at him, then bent down and picked up a backpack off the floor. "You have to put this on your back." Liam took the bag, but glanced at the storage box attached at the back of the scooter. "That's already full," Blaine said, following Liam's gaze.

Liam was dying to know what this was all about. However, he knew Blaine wouldn't tell him before they actually arrived at the super secret surprise place, so he didn't even bother asking.

Blaine put his own helmet on as he got on the Vespa, secured his phone in the holder on one of the handles, and jerked his head for Liam to get on behind him.

"Hold on tight," Blaine said as he turned the ignition on, and they seamlessly merged into the traffic.

Blaine drove smoothly, and Liam relaxed behind him as the navigation took them on picturesque roads up the hills, then down, the magnificent view of the ocean in the twilight mesmerising Liam. He couldn't look away. His eyes followed the water after every turn, every dip and curve in the road.

All too soon, Blaine parked the Vespa in front of an iron gate, turning the engine off.

"You have reached your destination," the navigation announced right before Blaine turned it off.

"Sooo," Liam drawled, removing his helmet and looking around. There was a house behind the gate, but it was dark, and it didn't seem like there was anyone around. "Where are we?"

"We are not where we're supposed to be yet," Blaine said with a smirk.

"Blaine..." Liam began, exhaling loudly. He was getting hungry again, the sandwich he'd had before he left the hotel a distant memory.

"Relax, babe," Blaine said, taking the helmet out of his hand and kissing him. "We're going to leave Betsy here, but we have to take the backpack and the supplies from the box with us."

"Betsy? You named the scooter?" Liam asked, raising an eyebrow.

"Doesn't she look like a Betsy to you?"

"No, Blaine, *it* looks like a blue scooter to me."

"Don't listen to him, honey," Blaine cooed, patting the Vespa on the handle. "You're a Betsy through and through."

Liam rolled his eyes, shouldered the backpack and folded his arms, waiting for Blaine to get the other bag out of the box.

"Come on," Blaine said, waving Liam over and wrapping an arm around his shoulders.

They walked down a narrow path that ran along the iron fence around the house, and after a few turns found themselves on a tiny beach. Liam gasped as he saw it, the golden sand twinkling in the full moon and the little waves rippling on the shore.

"What is this place?" Liam asked, looking around. "Are we supposed to be here? Isn't that a private beach for that house up there?"

"Yes, it is, and yes, we have permission to be here." Blaine smiled at him, then stepped closer and kissed him, slowly, sucking Liam's lower lip into his mouth. "We can stay here all night if we want."

Liam opened his mouth to ask how they were supposed to stay the night if they didn't have anywhere to sleep, when Blaine kissed him again until all thoughts flew out of his head. He clutched at Blaine's t-shirt, pulling him closer, wanting to feel all of Blaine all at once, and nothing else mattered.

"Relax, okay? I have it all under control." Blaine pulled away and walked down the beach towards the water, pulling Liam behind him.

Liam watched, fascinated, as Blaine started taking things out of the bags. First came a folded pop-up tent that he set up with flourish, then some blankets and finally containers with food. He spread one of the blankets inside the tent, folding the other as a pillow and propping it against the back, and the third he kept folded to the side. The tent was really small, Liam doubted they'd both fit in there, but thankfully the weather was warm, the sky was clear and they could lie down with their legs stretching outside the tent and still be comfortable.

"Alright, come sit down," Blaine said when he'd finished preparing everything.

Liam joined him on the blanket inside the tent, ridiculously touched that Blaine'd gone through all this trouble for him. He couldn't stop grinning as Blaine opened the plastic containers and offered Liam a variety of snacks, fruit and vegetables, all cut and seasoned to perfection.

Liam wolfed down everything Blaine gave him, and they finished everything in the containers in record time. Liam was a little worried that they didn't have any food left, but he didn't voice his concerns.

"There's more food in the backpack if you want," Blaine said, winking at Liam who looked at him sheepishly.

"Thanks, I'm alright. Maybe later."

They put everything safely away in the bags and lay down in the tent, facing each other, their arms and legs tangled together. As Liam'd predicted, their legs were sticking out of the kids' size tent, but he didn't care. The whole night was so well thought out and so romantic that a little detail like that only made it more memorable.

"Thank you," Liam said, his breath mingling with Blaine's, their lips nearly touching as they lay in each other's arms.

Blaine smiled, brushing Liam's nose with his. "My pleasure." He kissed him then, softly, lips tasting lips, no rush or expectation. “Oh,” he said, interrupting their kiss. “Something I should have said this morning.”

Liam met his eyes, wanting Blaine to stop talking already and kiss him again.

“What?”

“Happy birthday.”

Liam’s eyes widened in surprise. “You knew?”

“Yeah.”

“But how?”

“You wouldn't tell me so I had to do a little digging on my own. You didn't think I’d just forget that your birthday was coming up, did you?”

Liam shrugged, but didn't say anything. He never thought of his birthday as a big deal and it hadn’t even occurred to him that someone would be that interested in finding out the date, and surprising him like this.

“You did all this for my birthday?” Liam asked.

“Well, yes, and because you were upset and I couldn’t just stand there watching as you shrank into yourself.”

Liam’s throat tightened and he didn't trust himself to speak. Lowering his lashes, trying to hide the wetness in his eyes, he kissed Blaine again, deepening the kiss the moment their lips met. Blaine moaned softly, pulling Liam’s hips closer, their groins grinding together. He was as hard as Liam and just as eager to move things along.

"Baby," Blaine, said between kisses. "I'd like to ask you something."

Oh, God, Liam didn't want to talk or answer any questions or even think. He made a noise at the back of his throat, claiming Blaine's mouth again, not giving him a chance to speak.

Blaine pushed him gently away, cupping his cheek.

"Stop for a second, okay? This is important."

Liam groaned, untangling from Blaine and turning on his back. "Ask away," he said, barely keeping his annoyance at bay.

"I want you to fuck me," Blaine whispered, right in Liam's ear, his lips brushing the earlobe as they moved.

Liam turned his head sharply to look at Blaine and see if he was serious. Blaine was staring at him with hooded eyes, running his tongue over his lower lip.

"Why?" Liam blurted.

Blaine chuckled. "Why? Why the hell not?"

"Are you doing this just because it's my birthday? Is it part of the surprise?" Liam asked, without taking a moment to consider his words.

"No," Blaine said softly, reaching a hand to stroke Liam's cheekbone. "I've been thinking about it, *a lot*, ever since that first night we were together, and I really want it, Liam. I haven't done this in a very long time, but I want it with you."

Liam sank his teeth into his lip, overwhelmed with everything he was feeling right now.

"I really want it with you, too," he said, meeting Blaine's eyes.

"Good," Blaine murmured before cupping Liam's neck and bringing him in for a kiss.

Liam moved to straddle Blaine's hips without breaking their kiss, feeling Blaine smile against his mouth. He pulled his t-shirt over his head, leaning back down to meet Blaine's lips, as he worked Blaine's own t-shirt up his body. Blaine took over and quickly removed it, running his hands greedily over Liam's chest.

Liam bent down, propping himself on his hands on both sides of Blaine's head, and rolled his hips, grinding their cocks together through their jeans. Moaning, Blaine arched his back and dug his fingers in Liam's skin. Liam touched the tip of his tongue to Blaine's stubbled jaw, enjoying the roughness against his soft tongue. Tracing a wet line down his throat, Liam slid lower, playing with Blaine's nipples when he reached them. Blaine seemed to like that, burying his hands in Liam's hair, his breaths coming out in excited gasps.

Liam continued teasing him, licking his way down Blaine's body, tracing the muscles with his tongue, nipping at the skin, placing open mouthed kisses on Blaine's hipbones as he worked his jeans open.

Blaine eagerly helped with getting rid of the rest of his clothes, lying back down, naked and hard, his cock throbbing on his belly. Liam could look at him all night. The light dusting of hair on his chest, the darker happy trail down to his navel, that thick, perfect cock all his for the taking.

"Get undressed and fuck me already," Blaine said, his voice husky with need. He wrapped and hand around the base of his shaft and squeezed, closing his eyes in concentration. "I'm so close already, babe."

Liam liked having Blaine this turned on and entirely at his mercy. He grinned evilly, bending down to lick the length of Blaine's cock, then suck on the head, tasting the salty precome.

"Liam," Blaine growled in warning, his hips lifting off the blanket to fuck into Liam's mouth.

Liam pushed him back down, keeping him steady with a hand on his hip, gently sucking and licking his cock, enjoying the desperate sounds Blaine made. There wasn't enough friction for him to come, Liam made sure of that, but he wanted to drive Blaine incoherent with need. He wanted him to come the moment Liam was inside him, and keep coming as he fucked him.

He wanted him to forget everyone else he'd ever been with.

Blaine chanted a litany of curses, his skin glistening with sweat in the moonlight. Liam moved his attention lower to Blaine's balls, running his tongue over them, sucking each of them in his mouth. They were drawn tight, ready to explode, and Liam knew it was time to stop teasing or this whole seduction routine would have been for nothing.

He made quick work of the rest of his clothes, finding the condoms and lube in the front pocket of the backpack and prepared himself with swift determination. Blaine watched him, his blue eyes dark under heavy lids, lips wet and swollen from their kisses. He was so beautiful, so sexy, so incredibly perfect that Liam's stomach tightened with an uncomfortable, unwelcome feeling.

Before Blaine could sense Liam's hesitation, he crawled between his legs, pushing them as far apart as they would go, slick fingers massaging his hole. Blaine bowed off the blanket at the first touch on his sensitive skin, then rolled his hips around Liam's finger, silently asking for more. He was so tight that Liam was afraid he might hurt him, but the noises Blaine made spoke to the exact opposite. Liam added a second finger, squeezing some more lube on them, working Blaine open.

"Liam..." Blaine said urgently, hissing when Liam removed his fingers.

Lowering himself on top of Blaine, Liam kissed him, slowly, their tongues tangling playfully, their lips moving seamlessly together as if choreographed. He tried to stop thinking and just feel, but feeling wasn't any better. Liam was falling apart and it was all Blaine's fault.

"Ready?" Liam asked, the head of his cock slowly pushing inside Blaine.

Blaine nodded jerkily, grabbing Liam's hips and pulling him closer. Liam gasped when that made him bury himself inside Blaine in one stroke, the sensation suddenly overwhelming. Blaine was tight, and hot, and smooth, and it felt so fucking good to be inside him.

Liam rested his forehead against Blaine's, giving him a moment to adjust to his cock. Blaine was breathing heavily, his body shaking, his fingers leaving red marks on Liam's skin. Liam couldn't remember seeing Blaine so vulnerable, and the thought that he'd done that sent an uncomfortable twinge in his chest.

He needed to move, needed to feel physical pleasure in order to stop feeling anything else.

Propping himself on his hands, Liam met Blaine's eyes. They were full of so many emotions that something inside Liam broke. He couldn't do this right now, couldn't give himself over like that, not again.

Bending down and burying his face in the crook of Blaine's shoulder so that he didn't have to look at him anymore, Liam started moving, slowly at first, but quickly speeding up. Blaine wrapped his legs tightly around Liam's hips, and his arms around his waist, and held on while Liam fucked him, mindlessly chasing his pleasure.

"Liam... baby..." Blaine gasped out the words, his throat working as he swallowed thickly. "Fuck, that's good."

Liam felt Blaine's hand sneak between their bodies and it only took him a few strokes before he was coming, his ass pulsing around Liam's cock, and his whole body trembling as he milked every last drop of his cock. Liam wasn't too far behind, barely holding it together as it was. He let go, feeling the warm sensation of his orgasm spread through his body as he kept moving inside Blaine, unable to catch his breath.

Blaine held him tight even when Liam relaxed on top of him, his softening cock still inside him. His heart beat erratically against his chest, and he was sure Blaine could feel it too. Maybe that was why Blaine stroked his hair, and rubbed his back, and whispered calming words in his ear.

Soon, Liam's heart rate steadied, and he felt he should move before he crushed Blaine completely. Getting up, Liam rummaged through the bag until he found some wet wipes to clean themselves with, and unfolded the extra blanket. He disposed of the condom, wiped his belly as best as he could, then crouched down next to Blaine to clean him too. That done, he lay back down, wrapping the blanket around their naked bodies, cuddling close to Blaine.

The night was perfect – the breeze from the ocean cooled their hot skin, while the sound from the crashing waves brought magic to the night. The scattered lights from the *favelas* on the hills seemed like the sky had leaked twinkling stars and spread them all around.

It was beautiful, and magical, and everything Liam had ever wanted.

“Liam?” Blaine said softly, drawing his wandering thoughts back to the present.

“Hm?”

“Was Rio everything you imagined it would be?”

Liam propped himself on his elbow and turned to look at Blaine. He sensed that the question was loaded with deeper meaning that Blaine was letting on, but in the dim light he couldn't read Blaine's expression.

“Yes,” Liam finally said. “It was everything I imagined, and so much more.”

“So...” Blaine began, looking away. “You’ll miss it when we go back home?”

Liam frowned. “Of course I’ll miss it.”

Where was Blaine going with this?

“What if you don't have to?”

This conversation was getting weirder by the second.

“Blaine, whatever’s on your mind just spit it out.”

Blaine took a deep breath, his chest rising then quickly falling as he exhaled.

“I have an idea how you can stay here forever,” he said, holding Liam’s eyes uncertainly.

Liam smiled widely, thinking Blaine was joking. "Yeah? What is it?"

Blaine didn't smile back. "You know how in London you spend all your money on rent, bills, and travel, maybe a night out on the weekends and a shopping trip here and there, but there's rarely anything left at the end of the month? And then on top of that you're stuck in a job you don't really like, commute an hour in a crowded train two times a day, and your life is so different from what you imagined it would be that you barely even remember what you dreamed about in the first place?"

"If you're trying to make me depressed it's working," Liam said with a huff, laying his head back on Blaine's chest.

Blaine fingers dug into his scalp, massaging the sensitive skin and playing with his hair.

"I'm not trying to make you depressed. I'm saying, you have nothing to go back to London for."

"And what do you suppose I do here? How will I support myself if I don't even speak the language?"

"Social media," Blaine said, his voice devoid of any humour whatsoever.

Liam laughed, raising his head to look Blaine in the eyes, needing to make sure he wasn't, in fact, joking.

"What? Are you insane? What are you talking about?"

“Hear me out.” Blaine raised a hand to silence any protests, so Liam closed his mouth, sighed and motioned for him to continue. “We can create a travel and lifestyle blog. That would give us an opportunity to travel all over the world and get paid to do it. We can focus on different things, like how gay friendly a place is or how easy it is to travel with your pet or how much to tip in the local currency. We’ll gather all this info and make it easily accessible on the blog. Apart from that we can also write for travel magazines and do talk shows and YouTube corroborations. We’ll use all social media, not to just popularise our blog, but make a brand of ourselves, bringing in ad contracts and promotional opportunities. Thousands of people are doing that, Liam, and we can, too. We can live the life we want, here in Rio, or anywhere else in the world.”

Blaine cut himself off abruptly, biting the inside of his cheek as he watched Liam, who was stunned into silence. He didn't know how to react. Obviously, Blaine wasn’t joking. He'd put way too much thought into this, and the way he spoke about it made it clear he’d researched his ideas and truly believed they could be achieved.

But all Liam could focus on was one word.

“We?” Liam said, his throat tightening again.

“Well, yeah.” Blaine averted his eyes. “I thought we could do it together. If you want.”

“You’d leave your entire life in London to stay here in Rio with me, running a blog?”

Blaine shrugged. “I would. If you want me here I wouldn't think twice about it.”

Liam took a deep breath and lay back down, listening to Blaine's heart thumping in his chest. He didn't know what to say, so he kept silent, hoping Blaine would just forget about all this and they could sleep. In the morning, they’d laugh it off, and blame it all on their post-orgasmic scattered brains.

“Say something,” Blaine said, his voice barely above a whisper.

So, they weren’t letting this go. Okay, then.

“Blaine,” Liam began, sitting up to look at him. “This idea may sound absolutely amazing, but it’s also as far away from reality as humanly possible. I can’t just leave everything I’ve worked so hard for and move to Rio, hoping to make a living by running a travel blog.”

“Why not? We have no kids, no responsibility to anyone but ourselves. We can do anything we want, and that’s a luxury not many people have.”

Liam threw his hands in the air. There was that word again: we. What happened to casual? What happened to enjoying a holiday fling with no strings attached?

“Can we talk about this tomorrow?” Liam asked, laying back down. “I’m really tired, I can’t think straight right now. And I really don't want to argue with you.” He wrapped an arm around Blaine’s waist and exhaled in relief when Blaine drew him close and kissed the top of his head. "Tonight was perfect, Blaine. I'll never forget this night," Liam whispered, closing his eyes. His heart ached but he had to cut this in the bud or it would hurt so much more later on. "But our holiday ends in a few days, and so does this fantasy."

Blaine didn't reply. He just stroked up and down Liam's arm until he fell asleep.

Chapter fourteen

They didn't discuss it any further the next morning. Blaine took one look at Liam's guarded expression and knew he wouldn't achieve anything if he pushed the issue. So he smiled a lazy morning smile, manoeuvred Liam underneath him and kissed him, feeling the tension leaving Liam's body. They made love in the crisp morning air, the ripple of the waves and the cries of the seagulls the only sounds around them, apart from their panting breaths and soft words.

After, they held each other, both of them quiet and lost in their own thoughts. Blaine knew what Liam's biggest issue was – that single little word that meant everything to Blaine. *We*. He could do this on his own, of course he could, and he'd be lying if he said he hadn't considered leaving London and starting over somewhere new after his marriage fell apart. But now he wanted to do it with Liam, wanted to share every future adventure with this stubborn, beautiful man he'd fallen desperately in love with.

Blaine'd carefully considered every angle before pitching his idea to Liam. It wasn't like they didn't know what they were doing. They both had experience in the media, they knew how to work an audience, how to write engaging articles, and they both had connections. Liam's photos were gorgeous and would keep getting better the more he practised. They were both single, educated, smart guys in their twenties, with nothing tying them down to one place. Yeah, they'd miss their families and their friends, but in all honesty, how often did they see them anyway? And was it worth missing great opportunities in life only to stay close to your family?

The world was there at their feet, ready for the taking, and the only hurdle in their path was one little word.

We.

Blaine knew he'd sprung this on Liam when he'd least expected it, and more importantly, after feeding him some nonsense about not being ready for a relationship, and keeping things casual. He knew it wasn't fair to blindside him like this, or to ask him to make a decision when he was still drunk on Rio. He probably needed some time in the real world to think things over.

So Blaine would give him time. He wasn't giving up on his idea, on *them*, but he wouldn't mention anything until Liam was ready to discuss it.

They had a few of days left of their holiday, so he'd make sure they'd make the most of it.

They spent the last days of their holiday mostly sleeping in, lounging on the beach, eating ice-cream, and making love. Blaine never mentioned their conversation in the tent again, and soon Liam relaxed. The silences became comfortable again, the smiles bigger and the kisses longer. The ticking clock on their time together couldn't be paused, and Blaine could hear every tick and every tock in his mind, a countdown to the finish line. If Liam felt the same way, he didn't let on. He seemed happy, if a little melancholy about leaving Rio soon, but mostly he was full of smiles, silly jokes, and very naughty ideas of what he could do to Blaine in bed.

On their last day in Rio, after gathering their luggage and getting ready for the early morning flight the next day, Liam suggested they go out clubbing. The night started with a few drinks at the beach bar, then dancing and a few more drinks at a gay club. Blaine was sure they'd both regret this in the morning, especially with an eleven hour flight ahead of them, but he didn't care. Watching Liam as he danced, his movements graceful and free, his grin never leaving his face, Blaine knew the fierce hangover would be worth it.

"I need some fresh air," Blaine said in Liam's ear, catching his hand and dragging him off the dance floor and outside the club.

The silence outside was deafening after the thumping music inside, and Blaine was momentarily taken aback by the quiet of the night. The crisp night felt good on his flushed skin, clearing the fog on his mind a little.

Liam stepped closer to him, backing him against the wall, planting his hands on the sides of Blaine's head and caging him in.

"Fresh air?" He said, arching an eyebrow.

Blaine lunged forward and fused their mouths together, the desire he felt for Liam, the need to be with him, overpowering all his other thoughts. He threw caution to the wind, picking Liam up, turning and slamming his back against the wall. Liam grunted, but didn't protest, wrapping his legs around Blaine's waist, his arms around Blaine's neck, holding on as if he was never letting go.

But that wasn't true, was it?

Blaine kissed him desperately, possessively, bruising his lips with his stubble, with his teeth, claiming Liam's mouth as if it was his soul.

"I want you," Blaine panted against Liam's mouth, kissing him over and over, and unable to stop whatever was about to spill out of his mouth.

"You have me," Liam said, arching his back against the wall, searching for more friction on his hard cock.

"No, I don't." Blaine bit Liam's jaw, harder than he should have, but when Liam whimpered with need he nipped at it again, going all the way down his neck to his collarbone.

"Of course you do," Liam whispered, his voice husky with arousal. "I'll let you fuck me right here if that's what you need."

Blaine pulled away sharply, untangling Liam's legs from his waist and caging him in against the wall. Their faces were inches apart as they studied each other in the dim light of the street lamp. Liam's skin was hot, his cheeks pink with arousal, his mouth wet from Blaine's kisses. He was beautiful, and right here, in Blaine's arms, but it felt like he was slipping away, just out of reach.

"I don't need to fuck you against the wall of a night club, Liam," Blaine said, fanning his fingers on Liam's cheek. "I need you. I don't just mean right now. I want you in my life when we step out of that plane tomorrow. I want everything with you, not just a holiday fling."

Liam swallowed a few times, his Adam's apple moving against his skin, but he didn't say anything. His eyes grew guarded and Blaine felt the door slamming in his face.

It was now or never.

"I'm in love with you, Liam."

Liam sucked in a sharp breath, his eyes widening, but he still remained quiet. Too quiet.

"Fucking say something," Blaine whispered, resting his forehead against Liam's.

"I can't do this," Liam said, his voice catching on the last word.

"Why the fuck not? We're good together, baby."

Liam pushed Blaine away, making no apologies when Blaine stumbled backwards.

"Anyone would be good together here, Blaine!" Liam shouted, spreading his arms wide. "This is a fantasy, an exotic paradise that can lure anyone into thinking they're in love, that their dreams could become a reality, that what they're feeling is real. But it's not. It's a beautiful lie..."

"Don't tell me how I feel," Blaine interrupted him, his voice low. "I've been in love with you before we ever set foot in this 'fantasy'." He made air quotes with his fingers, stalking towards Liam and stopping right in front of him, meeting his furious gaze with his own.

"What are you talking about?" Liam folded his arms. "You said you weren't ready for a relationship and you were fine with casual. Which statement am I supposed to believe, Blaine?"

"I only said that because that was what you wanted to hear, and I didn't want to make this trip awkward for you. But I can't keep lying to myself, and to you." Blaine pulled Liam in his arms, palming his neck and bringing his mouth in for a kiss. Liam didn't resist. He let Blaine in without a fight, kissing him back as if that was their last kiss and he wanted to make the most of it.

"I. Love. You," Blaine said, enunciating every word, then kissing Liam again, not giving him a chance to protest.

"I can't do this," Liam said again as their lips separated. "It's not real," he whispered, barely audible.

Blaine felt his heart breaking into a million little shards.

Letting go of Liam, he stepped back, rubbing his chest with his palm. He wanted to cry, and scream, and punch the wall repeatedly until the physical pain dulled the ache in his chest.

But he didn't.

"Fine," was all he said before he turned on his heel and walked away from Liam.

"Blaine!" Liam called after him. "Where are you going?"

Blaine didn't stop. Didn't turn around. He kept walking and didn't much care where he would end up.

Chapter fifteen

Hearing the door open, Liam jumped out of bed and hurried towards Blaine. He hadn't come back to their room all night, and Liam hadn't slept a wink worrying about him.

"Where the fuck have you been?" Liam said, folding his arms, still clutching his phone in his hand. "I tried calling you a hundred times. Do you know how dangerous it is to wander around Rio de Janeiro alone at night, especially when you don't know the city?"

Blaine looked at him, his expression carefully hidden behind a mask of bored indifference. His eyes were red and he smelled like alcohol and cigarettes. Liam wrinkled his nose.

"You're a selfish bastard, you know that?" Liam stared him down, getting more and more angry.

"I can say the same about you," Blaine said, walking past him.

"What is that supposed to mean?"

Blaine shook his head and stalked into the bathroom without another word. Liam heard the lock turn with finality.

As angry as Liam was, he'd still felt his knees melt with relief when he'd seen Blaine was alright. All night he'd stared at the ceiling, dialling his number over and over again, imagining all the gruesome things that could happen to him. To his horror, his eyes prickled with tears of relief, and then a tidal wave of regret nearly drowned him.

He didn't want to fight with Blaine. When he'd told him he loved him Liam's heart had expanded in his chest to a point of bursting, and he wanted, more than anything, for those words to be true. He wanted to believe that Blaine meant what he'd said, and he also wanted to say it back, because somewhere along the way Liam had fallen for Blaine, too.

But the nagging thought at the back of his mind that this was all a fantasy, a screwed up version of reality that would come crashing down on them the moment they set foot in London, remained. What they had here was easy. It was fun and romantic and magical. But it couldn't last.

Could it?

Liam sat on the bed, burying his face in his hands. God, he was tired. Physically, mentally, just really fucking tired of the whirlwind of emotions messing with his head. He needed some time away from Blaine, away from Rio's enchanting charisma, to think all this through, get a clear perspective and figure out what the hell he was going to do.

Because right now it seemed like he was hurting the guy he loved, going back to a job he hated and throwing away every opportunity the universe was serving him on a silver platter.

The shower turned off, and soon enough Blaine emerged from the bathroom, a towel around his waist. He didn't make eye contact as he walked around the room, gathering any of his things that remained lying around, and dumping them in his suitcase.

"Blaine?" Liam said, but Blaine ignored him.

Liam stood up, walking to him and standing directly in his way. Blaine raised his eyes to him, but didn't say anything.

"Look," Liam began, running a hand through his hair. "I don't want to fight with you." Blaine's eyes softened but he didn't move. "I..."

I love you, too, he wanted to say. *I want this, us, to work out, but I'm scared as fuck. I'm hurting inside, just like you, and I'm sorry.*

"I need some time, okay?" he said instead, averting his eyes, afraid that Blaine would see right through him.

"Okay," was all Blaine said, but his voice was gentle, and it gave Liam hope that maybe he hadn't fucked this up for good.

The trip back was fucking awkward. Blaine rarely said anything, or acknowledged when Liam tried to talk to him. In the end, Liam had given up, letting the silence hang between them, filled with all the words they couldn't – wouldn't – say.

At Heathrow, they collected their bags, cleared customs and passport control, and walked out the airport, shivering in the cool evening air, their bodies not yet acclimated to London temperatures. Liam was exhausted after the long flight and all he wanted was to curl in his bed and sleep for a week. Unfortunately, he was due back to work the very next day. The thought deepened the feeling of despair he already felt. Leaving Rio behind had been hard, but going their separate ways with Blaine would be even harder.

"So, I guess this is it?" Blaine said, jarring Liam out of his thoughts.

Turning to look at him, Liam opened and closed his mouth a few times, his brain refusing to cooperate. He wanted to say so many things, but he was tired, and he was afraid of fucking things up even more if he opened his mouth and the wrong thing came out.

Blaine nodded, as if reading his thoughts. "See you around, Liam," he said with quiet resignation, cupping his cheek and brushing a thumb over Liam's cheekbone.

When he turned his back on him and walked away, Liam felt something inside him shatter. A heavy weight settled on his chest, nausea building up in his stomach.

But the worst of it all was the gut feeling that he'd never see Blaine again, never feel his touch or taste his lips.

No, the worst of it all was that he'd held everything he'd ever wanted in his hands, and then stupidly let it all go.

Chapter sixteen

The bar Liam's friends had dragged him to was weird. It was hidden underneath a juice bar in Covent Garden, and they had to walk down a winding staircase, Becky tripping in her high heels and nearly dragging Stewart and Liam down as she lost her balance. Thankfully, they all made it in one piece to the bar, where they were shown to their table by a polite hostess, assuring them their barman will be with them soon.

"Our barman will come to our table? Did I hear that right?" Liam asked, taking off his jacket and hanging it on the back of his chair.

Both Stewart and Becky looked at him wide-eyed as if he'd said he'd never seen Game of Thrones.

"You've never been here before?" Asked Stewart. Liam shook his head. "It's the trendiest bar in London right now, mate." Sitting down, he took a bottle of vodka from his bag and set it on the table. "We bring our own alcohol and a barman prepares custom made cocktails for us on the spot."

Becky nodded enthusiastically, her big blue eyes scanning the bar.

"What? Seriously? You bring your own booze and you still pay for your drinks?" Liam failed to see the logic in the whole concept.

"It's all part of the theme," Becky said with a wave of her hand. "It's a speakeasy from the 1920s during the prohibition, so they can't sell alcohol."

Liam wanted to argue that they could have drinks at any bar in Covent Garden without having to carry a bottle of vodka around, probably for the same price, but decided against it. Bring-your-own-booze concept aside, the bar was really nice. It was a bit too dark, the only light coming in from colourful jars with candles inside scattered all around. But the décor was tasteful and very retro with wood panelling on the walls, a real stone fireplace in the far wall, and an antique piano in the corner. The music wasn't so loud that they couldn't have a proper conversation without shouting, but loud enough to fill any uncomfortable silences.

His friends had been pestering him to go out with them ever since he'd come back from Rio, but he wasn't feeling up to it until now. In all honesty, he wasn't feeling up to it right now either, but it was that or have them storm his flat and refuse to leave. At least this way he could go home any time he wanted.

"Sooo," Stewart drawled, leaning back in his chair and waggling his eyebrows. "Tell us about your hot boyfriend."

"He's not my boyfriend."

"Oh, please, we've all seen the pictures on social media. You're pretty much celebrities right now."

Liam snorted. “Hardly.”

The barman arrived then, pushing a trolley with all kinds of bottles on it, as well as pots of fresh herbs and a whole tray of sliced fruit. He was really charming, asking each of them what they liked in their cocktails and suggesting several combinations until they chose their perfect blend.

Drinks in hand, they watched as the barman moved on to the next table, which was thankfully further away than the cramped tables in most London bars. Liam really didn’t want anyone overhearing their conversation.

Becky and Stewart voiced their appreciation of the cocktails, then stared at Liam expectantly, and he had a feeling they wouldn’t want to change the subject before he told them everything.

So, he did.

He told them about Rio, about Blaine, about falling stupidly in love when he’d promised himself he wouldn't do it, about the jellyfish sting, and Blaine’s surprise for his birthday, and his idea for travelling the world together. About Blaine telling him he loved him and Liam’s refusal to believe he meant it.

The moment he was done, both his friends started talking over each other. Phrases like ‘fucking stupid’, ‘bloody idiot’, and ‘are you insane?’ were the most common in their tirade. Fed up with being yelled at, Liam excused himself and practically ran to the toilets.

Locking himself in one of the stalls, Liam hung his head in his hands and took a few deep breaths. He knew his friends meant well, but hearing someone else say out loud what he already knew made it all too real.

To his horror, Liam felt burning behind his eyes and sure enough, a lone tear rolled down his cheek. The last thing he wanted to do was cry, locked in the toilet of the trendiest bar in London on a Saturday night, but it seemed like he couldn't control his own emotions anymore. He was exhausted, barely sleeping at night, staying up late to listen to Blaine's show. When he closed his eyes, Liam could imagine Blaine right there, next to him, talking only to him. Sometimes he could swear he felt Blaine's fingers in his hair, the scent of his skin on the pillow.

It was pathetic, and Liam knew it, but he couldn't do anything about it. The thought of going to bed without having Blaine's voice lull him to sleep was unbearable.

The two weeks since he'd come back had crawled like a snail in slow motion. Liam felt as if it'd been two years, the memory of the trip so distant as if it'd happened to someone else.

The days dragged monotonously, making Liam even more annoyed at work than he already was. Jenny, the girl he was usually on shift with, watched him like a hawk, probably afraid Liam would go off on someone soon, or do something really stupid. Like give his fucking two weeks' notice and get out of this dead end job.

She was a nice girl, pretty, polite, and always brought him back a bar of chocolate or a chai latte when she went on her lunch break. Liam didn't leave his desk anymore, didn't take any lunch breaks or even a trip to the vending machine. What was the point? He wasn't hungry or had any desire to do anything.

The door of the toilets opened, then closed with a creak, startling Liam. He was drowning in his misery, and he'd completely lost track of time. His friends were probably worried.

A knock sounded on the stall door, and Liam froze. He didn't want anyone to see him like this, but it was too late for that, wasn't it?

Wiping his eyes with the heels of his palms, Liam stood up and opened the door, coming face to face with Stewart. His friend took one look at Liam before gathering him in his arms.

"Oh, honey," he said, patting his back. "I'm sorry. Becky and I were too harsh, weren't we?"

Liam pulled away, heading for the sinks. "It's not that," he said, opening the cold water tap. "I *am* an idiot, and I know it."

Stewart came to stand next to him, watching him in the mirror, the concern in his warm dark eyes making the knot in Liam's gut twist even tighter. He splashed his face with cold water, grabbing a paper towel from the dispenser. Drying himself off, Liam stared at his reflection, realising for the first time how awful he looked. He had bags under his eyes the size of Texas, his hair was longer than how he usually liked it, and his cheeks were hollow, as if he'd lost weight. Thinking about it, his jeans did feel a little loose this morning...

"Liam," Stewart said, waving a hand in front of Liam's face.

Liam stared at him blankly, not really sure why Stewart was annoyed with him again. It seemed like there was something he wanted to tell Liam, but decided not to, sighing with resignation.

"Let's just go back to our table. Becky and I will listen and not judge, I promise."

Somehow Liam doubted that, but he couldn't lock himself in the toilets for the rest of the night, could he?

Becky gave him a hug when they reached the table, and pointed at the fresh drinks.

"I got us a refill. Something tells me we're going to need it."

Liam thanked her and sipped from his drink, staring at the table.

"Have you called him since you got back?" Becky asked.

Liam shook his head. "No. We texted a couple of times, but not like before. He's distant, probably moved on already."

"I doubt that, considering he told you he loved you two weeks ago," Stewart said.

Liam lifted his eyes to meet Stewart's, considering his words.

"Maybe he has, maybe he hasn't, I don't know, because he won't talk to me like he used to."

Liam wanted to go home. Desperately. He wanted to stop talking, stop thinking, stop obsessing over something that just wasn't meant to be.

"Alright, look," Becky said, placing a hand on Liam's shoulder to get his attention. "Stewart and I both love you." She glanced at Stewart who nodded in agreement. "But you need to hear the harsh truth."

Liam groaned, not really up to hearing any harsh truths.

Becky continued, ignoring Liam's reluctance to listen.

"I get where you're coming from, I really do. And you were right to take a step back and think about everything with a clear head." Liam looked at her in surprise, the last thing he expected her to say was that she agreed with him. "But that's not what you've been doing. You've been wallowing in your own misery, feeling sorry for yourself, missing the man you *love* and not having the fucking balls to tell him that."

He should have known there was a 'but'.

"Look," Stewart took over, claiming Liam's attention. "That whole thing with the blog is not such a bad idea. We currently use several popular bloggers and

Instagram accounts to promote our new range, and the campaign has been really successful."

Liam considered this for a moment. Stewart worked at the marketing department of a health food company, manufacturing anything from diet drinks and ready-mixed protein shakes, to food supplements and energy bars.

Liam wasn't clueless – he did work at a lifestyle magazine – even if he was just a receptionist. He read the magazine every month plus half a dozen others. He knew YouTubers, bloggers, and Instagrammers were on the rise, getting offered book and TV deals left and right, and living a life of luxury and adventure. But these were the chosen few of all people who tried, and mostly failed, to use social media to make a living.

"But what if it doesn't work out?" Liam blurted out, voicing his biggest fear. "What if we move to Rio, start this whole thing, and nobody cares? What if we spend all our savings and we have no income coming in to cover our bills, and end up on the street?"

Stewart smirked, throwing a pointed look at Becky. Confused, Liam watched them both smile knowingly at each other, before Becky fixed him with her big blue eyes, and said,

"The fact that you're only worried whether your *business* venture will work out, speaks volumes, don't you think?"

"What else am I supposed to be worried about?" Liam was still confused as hell, especially now that they were both staring at him as if he was brain damaged.

"Your relationship!" The both said in unison, the high-fived each other before erupting in giggles.

"No more refills for you," Liam said, signalling to the hostess to bring them their bill.

"Don't you see?" Becky said, reaching for her drink. "You two are meant to be together, and deep down in your cold little heart you know it."

Chapter seventeen

The loud banging on Blaine's door made him jump and nearly spill his gin and tonic. He wasn't expecting anyone and the concierge hadn't buzzed anyone in for him, as far as he knew. Was it one of his neighbours? He wasn't friendly with anyone, but maybe they needed help?

The banging came again, and then the mystery of his late night caller was solved.

"Blaine, open the fucking door."

Placing his drink on the table, Blaine stood and padded to the door.

"Hayden," he said, letting his friend storm in. "How did you get past the concierge?" They always called him when he had a visitor, Blaine had especially requested it.

Hayden levelled him with a look. "Did you seriously just ask me that?"

"Never mind," Blaine mumbled, waving Hayden into the kitchen.

"Why haven't you been answering my calls?" Hayden demanded, plopping into a chair.

"Because I don't want to talk to you." Blaine dropped a piece of lemon into a glass, then added the gin and tonic before handing it to Hayden.

"And you hung up on me when I called you at work!" Hayden said, outraged, but accepting the drink anyway.

"You called me *on air*!"

"You should know me better than to think I'll just give up and drop it. I will always find a way to get the information I need."

"I'm not the subject of one of your articles, Hayden."

Blaine sat across from his friend, all the fight draining out of him. He didn't want to do this right now, on his night off, the night he'd set aside for getting drunk and forgetting about Liam at least for a little while.

"No, you're not," Hayden said, softly, reaching for Blaine's hand across the kitchen table. "You're my best friend. And I can't bear to see you like this, babe. It's pathetic."

"Thanks," Blaine mumbled, running a hand over his face.

He did feel pathetic, though. Apart from going to work every night, he barely left his flat. He tied to sleep, but always ended up staring at the ceiling. The little energy he had left he poured into his show, trying his best to act normal. If his colleagues had noticed he'd been acting weird ever since he got back from Rio, they never said anything, but Blaine caught his producer studying him intently a couple of times.

"Look, I can piece the story together by what I've seen and what you've told me already," Hayden said.

Blaine tried to remember exactly how much he'd told him. They'd texted a few times while he was in Rio, and he'd sent him that picture of Liam sleeping on his chest. And then of course, Blaine'd sent him an ill advised email telling him about his blog idea and asking his opinion.

"So you don't have to talk, but you'll listen and you'll listen carefully."

Blaine sat back in his chair, folding his arms. He was used to Hayden bossing him around – Hayden bossed everyone around – but he also knew his no nonsense friend would probably give him the best advice.

"As I said in the email, the blog idea sounds promising. I'll give you the push you need to get your foot in the door. I asked around and I already have a few contacts lined up who will be happy to give you a signal boost, so to speak."

Blaine was stunned into silence. He knew Hayden approved of the idea, but he never thought he'd actually help him turn this crazy venture into reality.

"So that's not a problem, don't worry about it," Hayden waved a hand dismissively, taking a sip of his drink. "Your real problem here is Liam. He doesn't trust that this outrageously alluring idea can be turned into a real business, correct?" Blaine nodded. "You need to gather your facts, babe. Collect all the data, research all aspects and turn it into a proposal he can't refuse. Show him he can trust you. Turning your life around in a blink of an eye is not easy, so you both need to know what you're doing." Blaine nodded again, the gears in his brain already turning.

Hayden's logical brain had picked the issue apart and found the most practical resolution, while Blaine had been mopping around, feeling sorry for himself for two weeks.

Blaine stood up, walked round the table to Hayden and picked him up from the chair in a bear hug. Hayden screeched, yelling for Blaine to put him down, but Blaine squeezed him harder.

"I love you so much right now," Blaine said, then dropped Hayden back down in the chair.

"You're such an ogre," Hayden grumbled, straightening his shirt.

"You make it too easy, weighing a hundred pounds and all."

"A hundred and fifty, thank you."

Blaine quirked an eyebrow, not believing for a second Hayden weighed that much.

"I wasn't finished, by the way," Hayden said with annoyance. "I realise you probably won't sleep all night making your Power Point presentation, but for this to work you need to bear in mind something else, too."

"What?"

"Do you know what he wants?" Hayden asked, his expression turning from focused to wickedly playful. "Do you know what *everyone* wants when they're making a life changing decision?"

Blaine frowned, racking his brain for any possible answer and coming up blank.

"A grand gesture," Hayden said, grinning at Blaine.

Hayden left soon after dropping the whole grand gesture bomb on Blaine, but refusing to give him any ideas. It was Blaine's job to figure out what to do in order to get Liam back.

He'd been right, of course. Blaine worked way past midnight to prepare everything for tomorrow, checking and double checking his facts, as well as planning his 'grand gesture' to the very last detail. By the time he was done Blaine was grinning like an idiot, imagining Liam's face when he saw what Blaine'd come up with. Imagining him wrapping his arms around Blaine's neck and saying 'yes'.

Because there was no other option. Blaine wasn't giving up even if he had to come up with a thousand grand gestures. He wasn't letting Liam go ever again.

His phone vibrated on the bed next to him just as Blaine was gathering all the papers and starting to get ready for bed.

Blaine's pulse quickened when he read the text from Liam. They hadn't said anything like that to each other ever since they'd walked their separate ways at the airport. The nagging feeling that Liam had never really had any feelings for him, that it was too fucking late, evaporated with three simple words.

Chapter eighteen

Liam saw the delivery guy walk into the building carrying a huge bouquet of flowers and a bright yellow balloon. He rolled his eyes before plastering a fake smile on his face as the guy reached the reception desk.

"I have flowers for Laura Hart," the guy said, looking at his clipboard. "And a balloon for Liam Young."

Liam heard Jenny gasp but he was too stunned to react. With his peripheral vision he saw her coming to his rescue, signing for the deliveries and wishing the guy a nice day.

"Liam!" She snapped, too close to his ear for comfort.

"Jesus, calm the fuck down," Liam said, his annoyance evaporating when he saw the hurt look in her eyes. "Sorry."

She smiled at him, too curious to see who was sending him a yellow, helium filled balloon at work to stay mad at him for long.

Liam pulled the balloon closer by the string inspecting it. When he turned it around he saw the words 'Holiday Bubble' written in big black letters, and 'pop' scrawled underneath framed in a dramatic explosion drawing.

"Pass me the scissors, please," Liam asked Jenny, who was staring wide-eyed at the balloon not really understanding what was going on.

"Was there a card? Who is it from?" She placed the scissors in Liam's outstretched hand, trying to look past him at the balloon.

"Nope," he replied, popping the balloon right in the middle of the 'pop' drawing. "No need for a card."

He grinned when the balloon burst open and a folded piece of paper fell out of it. His smile grew even bigger when he read the hand-written note.

Dear Liam,
You just popped our holiday bubble! For an exclusive sneak peek of what our life could be like outside of the holiday bubble, follow the clues.
Yours, always,
Blaine

P.S. Your first clue is hidden under a bench in Hyde Park.
P.P.S. I realise there're a lot of benches so I'll make it easier for you. It's the third one from the left on the north side of the Princess Diana memorial.

"I have to go," Liam threw over his shoulder, heading for the door.

"When will you be back?" Jenny called after him, but he was already walking out the building. He felt a bit guilty for leaving her alone without any warning, but it was a really slow day. They'd barely had anyone come in besides the delivery guy.

Liam couldn't wipe the smile off his face as he walked towards Hyde Park. Last night he'd made his mind to talk to Blaine, in person, and at least try to work things out between them. He'd been wrong – it'd never been just a holiday fling. What he felt for Blaine was real. Rio or not, he was in love with Blaine, and hoped Blaine still loved him, too.

He reached the Princess Diana memorial in record time, out of breath but exhilarated, adrenalin pumping in his veins. Counting the benches, Liam located the right one and headed towards it. There was an old lady sitting on one end, who looked at Liam suspiciously as he kneeled on the ground and started feeling under the bench.

His fingers found a piece of paper stuck to the bottom. Carefully peeling it off, Liam turned it around to take a look. It was a print out of a QR code.

Sitting on the bench, casting a look at the old lady who was still watching him carefully, probably considering calling the police by now, he took out his phone and scanned the code.

A website called 'Liam and Blaine's Holiday Bubble' popped on his screen announcing the website was under construction, but coming soon. There was, however, a picture of Liam and Blaine in their 80s attire from the night of the race. They looked ridiculously happy. Liam stroked the picture on the screen, the ache in his chest intensifying.

Looking around, he scanned the few people around the memorial for Blaine. He must be somewhere nearby, right? Liam wanted to see him so badly, bury his face in the crook of his neck and inhale the scent of his skin.

Returning his attention back to his phone, Liam noticed something written as a caption underneath the photo:

> Go to the bench right across the memorial. Your next clue is waiting for you there.

Liam all but ran towards the bench, crouching in front of it and peeling off a plastic file from underneath. It was heavy, a stack of papers inside. Liam sat down, opening the file and starting to read.

He shook his head, unable to believe Blaine'd done all that. In the file he'd collected all sorts of data, outlining their estimated income and expenses, plus average living and travel costs. He'd also drawn a plan of suggested topics to cover, places to visit, companies they could contact for endorsement deals, magazines and websites to get in touch with for publishing freelance articles.

There was a separate section for visiting friends and family, income from renting out Blaine's London flat, and how long they could afford to live off their savings without generating any revenue.

A hand written Post-It note on the bottom of the page said Blaine's producer wanted to talk to them both about doing a weekly guest show for the RPRM FM, and his friend Hayden had offered to help them get started.

Liam's head was spinning and he hadn't even read the whole thing yet. He had no idea there was so much they could do. It was a full time job, a business, an opportunity to do something with their lives, something they loved.

Liam thumbed through the rest of the document, scanning all the information Blaine'd written, but his mind racing too fast for him to absorb anything. He wanted to see Blaine, right now, wanted to hug him and tell him how much he loved him.

At the end of the document, a hand written line in thick, black ink caught his eye. It stood out among all the neatly types letters.

Turn around

Liam jumped off the bench and turned, his eyes locating Blaine immediately. He was walking towards him across the grass, carrying something in his arms, his grin so big that Liam could see it from where he was standing.

Without a second thought Liam ran, not stopping until he was right in front of Blaine.

“Hi,” he said, breathless from the run, but also from seeing Blaine after so long.

“Hey,” Blaine replied, his eyes roaming over Liam’s face as if seeing him for the first time. “You’ve lost weight,” he added with a frown.

Something moved in Blaine's arms and Liam looked at the bundle he was carrying. A fluffy black head poked from under the fleece blanket.

“And you have a puppy!” Liam reached for the dog and Blaine surrendered it without any hesitation.

“No, *you* have a puppy.”

Liam looked at Blaine sharply, trying to keep the wiggling bundle from falling, and comprehend Blaine’s words at the same time.

“What?”

“She’s yours. I got her for you. You can finally have the dog you always wanted.”

Liam’s eyes filled with tears. It was all too much, too big, too emotional.

“Are you serious?” He asked, speaking around a lump in his throat.

"Yeah." Blaine stepped closer, wrapping both Liam and the puppy in his arms. She settled down, content to lie in Liam's arms under the soft blanket. "I love you, Liam. And I want to spend the rest of my life with you, travelling the world, chasing new adventures, looking after our dog. I want to spend all my wild nights and lazy mornings with you. I want you, for as long as you want me, and I'll do anything for that to be forever."

Liam couldn't speak even if he wanted to. Tears were running down his cheeks and his throat had closed off. Heart thudding in his chest, he wet his lips, willing Blaine to kiss him. He didn't have to wait long before Blaine's lips found his, kissing him softly, as if for the first time.

Liam pulled away, finally finding his voice. "I love you, Blaine. And I want all this, too."

Blaine's smile was wide, and his eyes seemed suspiciously wet, but he didn't cry. He kissed Liam again, pulling him closer, but mindful of the puppy.

"What about her? How are we supposed to travel with her?" Liam asked.

"We'll take her when we can, and when we can't we'll find her a sitter or leave her with friends for a few days. She has a passport, but needs another injection before she can travel abroad."

Liam nodded, looking down at the puppy. She'd fallen asleep in his arms and Liam realised he'd fallen desperately in love with the tiny, fluffy bundle the moment he'd seen her.

"We'll need a couple of months to set everything in motion, and I want you to move in with me during that time. I can't stand to spend another night without you, baby."

Liam's eye prickled with the happiest tears he'd ever felt. Leaning in, he whispered, "Okay," then met Blaine's warm lips in a long, languid kiss.

"This is crazy," he said, when their lips separated.

"When was the last time you did something crazy?"

"When I called the radio, looking for a Jonathan Reed." Liam smiled fondly, remembering the moment he'd decided to do that.

The moment that had changed his life.

"And look how that turned out," Blaine said with a wink.

The puppy stirred, letting out a little snort as she settled in Liam's arms again.

"Do you know what you want to call her?" Liam asked, looking at the puppy's beautiful face. He gently caressed the top of her head with his finger, trying not to wake her.

"I have an idea, but I wanted you to choose."

"I have an idea, too."

"On three?"

Liam nodded, and when Blaine counted to three they both said,

"Rio!"

THE END

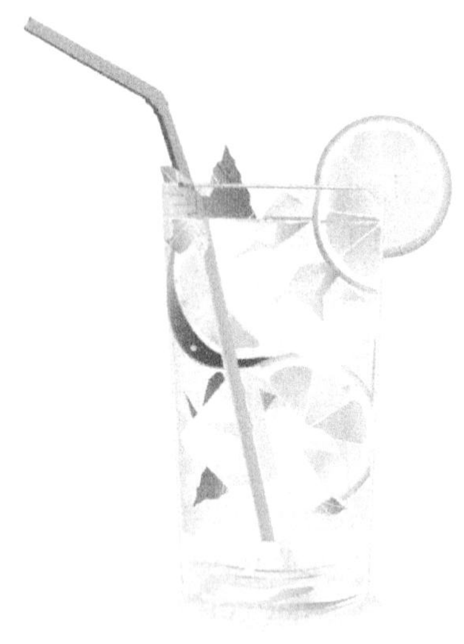

AUTHOR'S NOTE

This book was inspired by a true story. Well, several true stories, actually.

The first spark of an idea hit me when I was driving home one day, listening to the radio, and a woman called to ask if a man with a certain name would like to go on a luxury holiday to Thailand with her, because she'd broken up with her fiancé and would lose the holiday if both people didn't show up. By the end of the radio show, she'd found her travel companion. I don't know if their story was anything like Liam and Blaine's, but I'd like to imagine they had a good time together.

Intrigued, I did some research and discovered blogs, forums and message boards dedicated to people looking for stand-ins for non refundable holidays. So the idea didn't seem that unbelievable anymore.

The second true story is mine. When I started thinking about a fun, sexy summer novella, there was no question in my mind where the story would be set. I went to Rio two years ago and fell in love. I did all the things Liam and Blaine did, and in this book I tried to show how beautiful, how vibrant and unique Rio de Janeiro is. I feel like the city is as much a character in this story as Liam and Blaine.

The third spark of inspiration behind this book is a close friend of mine who turned his life around when his partner of eight years walked out on him without any warning. He sold everything he could, donated the rest, packed his bags and started travelling. In a year, he was generating a decent income from freelancing travel articles and endorsement deals, and was happily in love with someone else.

Happy endings do happen in real life. All we need is a little faith and a lot of courage.

ACKNOWLEDGEMENTS

With this book I hit every hurdle possible – computer crashing and deleting thousands of words; writer's block; big changes in my personal life diminishing my writing time; illness that took me weeks to recover from.

Many times I felt like I should just give up and move on to something else. But, miraculously, I didn't. I kept at it and managed to write THE END three months after the planned deadline.

What followed was a crazy last minute whirlwind of revisions, editing, proofing, promotion and organising everything else that needed to be done before release day. I couldn't do any of it if it wasn't for my friends who were eager to help with anything they could, reading the book in record time to give me feedback or do the final proofread in super short notice.

You know who you are.

Love you, guys! xx

ABOUT THE AUTHOR

Teodora is a bestselling, award winning author writing across genres, but has a soft spot for contemporary romance. As a passionate and vocal supporter of equal rights, LGBTQ+ themes are explored in most of her novels. A Creative Writing and English graduate, Teodora began writing full length novels in college, but only got the courage to show some of them to the world long after she graduated. She's now been published by several publishers in five languages, and has attended book signings around the world. She loves travelling, and her wanderlust has inspired several of her novels. Her other passion is musical theatre and she can often be found in London's West End trying to score a last minute ticket for a musical.

When she's not writing, Teodora loves watching anime, rearranging her enormous bookshelves or walking around London, always looking for a cosy, quirky coffee shop to settle in with her Kindle and a cup of tea.

Also by Teodora Kostova

West End series:

Dance

Mask

Dreaming of Snow

Piece by Piece

Heartbeat series:

In a Heartbeat

Then, Now, Forever

Cookies series:

Cookies

Grounded

Stand-alone novels:

Snowed In

Kiss and Ride

Ten Mile Bottom

CONTACTS

Website: www.teodorakostova.com
Amazon: www.amazon.com/author/teodorakostova
Twitter: @Teodora_Kostova
Facebook: www.facebook.com/teodorakostovaauthor
Facebook group: Teodora's Book Corner
https://www.facebook.com/groups/245720345600711/
Instagram: @teodorika1

Don't miss out on the latest news, events, book signings and giveaways! Visit my website and sign up for my newsletter!